Captain
Kempton's
Christmas

JAYNE DAVIS

Verbena
Books

Copyediting & proofreading: Sue Davison

ACKNOWLEDGEMENTS

Thanks to my critique partners on Scribophile for comments and suggestions, particularly David N, Daphne, Jim, Kim, Lynden, Sharon, and Violetta.

Thanks also to Alpha readers Tina, Trudy, Helen, Mary G and Dane, and Beta readers Barbara, Cilla, Dawn, Doris, Fran, Leigh, Melanie, and Wendy.

CHAPTER 1

December 23rd, 1814, Wiltshire

Captain Philip Kempton winced as he dismounted in front of the Blue Bell Inn. He'd been riding for hours and his back and legs ached. He shouldn't have been surprised—what had he expected after spending most of the last ten years at sea? It served him right, too. He'd barely mentioned the possibility of riding to Beechgrove when his mother launched into a lament about the cold weather, the state of the roads, and how he would be much more comfortable if he borrowed the chaise. Already irritated by the way she'd pressed him to accept the invitation from Aunt Beth and Uncle Thomas, he'd dug his heels in and insisted that his father's hunter would be the most comfortable way of making the journey. And he'd managed without a valet for a decade, thank you; his uncle's man could do anything needed over the festive season.

So here he was, still an hour's ride from his destination, with a backside that not even a hot bath would soothe, and fingers and toes numb from the chill air. The night would get colder still, he thought as he regarded the clear sky, its pale blue already turning a duskier shade. It would be dark by the time he arrived, but the moon was nearly full and would light his way. An hour spent thawing out in the inn would make little difference. The horse deserved a rest, too.

He walked into the inn, hoping his aching muscles didn't show in the way he moved. The stone-flagged passageway inside was dim, but a door stood ajar and Philip entered the heat and noise of the taproom. The air was thick with smells of woodsmoke, spilled ale, and unwashed bodies, the laughter raucous.

"What can I do for you, sir?" The landlord leaned in close and raised his voice to make himself heard above the hubbub.

Philip rubbed his face, the noise and smell almost making him regret his decision to halt here. But warming himself wasn't his only reason for stopping—he was still debating whether to just turn around and return home. He could think up some excuse and send Aunt Beth his regrets.

"Sir?"

He was here now, so he might as well eat. "Ale. And a hot meal."

"Very good, sir. We've a fish stew, or beef pie. Cook can do something else, if you wish, but you'd have to wait a bit."

"Beef pie will do nicely." It was too loud in here to think. "Do you have a private parlour that's warm?"

The man nodded. "Fire's lit in the room just across the hallway, sir. Send your food in there, shall I?"

"Yes, please do."

The parlour was furnished only with a couple of tables and chairs, and a high-backed settle near the fireplace. Philip threw a couple of extra logs onto the fire and stood with his back to the flames, hands behind him as if he was still on the quarterdeck of the *Penelope*. His fingers were warm and tingling by the time the landlord appeared, a maid with a laden tray behind him.

"Going far, sir?" the man said as the maid set out a plate with a huge slice of pie swimming in gravy, a dish of vegetables, and a mug of ale.

"Delfont Abbas," Philip said.

"Nice place; I come from there. Addison, at the Delfont Arms, brews a fine ale. Nearly as good as mine," he added, with a wink.

"I'm staying at Beechgrove, but no doubt I'll find time to test your recommendation."

"Friend of the family, sir?"

"Kempton's my uncle." Philip sat down, his stomach rumbling in anticipation.

"Ah, you'll be Captain Kempton, then. Addison and I have been following your actions in the papers. You've been making a splendid fight against the Frogs, sir."

"Yes, well…" Philip didn't know what to say—they'd all just been doing their duty.

"Enjoy your meal, Captain. It's on the house. Just shout if you want more ale."

Damn it—he was committed to spending Christmas at Beechgrove now. If the man was friendly with the landlord of the Delfont Arms, word would eventually reach his aunt and uncle that he'd been on his way.

It's been four years, he told himself—you should be over it by now. But flashes of that summer fortnight still came back to him when he couldn't sleep, or when he let his mind wander. Days of shared walks on the Downs or through the Beechgrove gardens. Days when he'd fallen in love with a woman who'd promised to wait for him.

And his thoughts always ended on the irony of being given command of a frigate named after a wife who *had* waited.

∿

Lady Anna Radnor huddled into her pelisse, trying to ignore her discomfort as the post chaise rattled and bumped along the road. It wasn't the winter chill that troubled her, for her hands were warm inside her fur muff and the hot brick from the last posting inn kept the chill from her feet. No, the problem was the large pot of tea she'd drunk an hour before. She wriggled again, but it was no use. She couldn't wait until they reached Beechgrove.

She rapped on the glass to attract the attention of the Kemptons' groom, riding on the nearside horse. The icy air made her eyes water as she dropped the side window.

"Stop at the next inn, if you please. How far is it, do you know?"

"Only a mile or so, my lady."

Anna drew the window up, snuggling into the cushions with appreciation. It was good of Aunt Beth to have sent the chaise for her. She had enough funds now to keep a carriage of her own, but she had little use for one, and habits of economy were sometimes hard to discard. Beth Kempton was no relation to her, but she had been a close friend of her mother and treated her like a niece.

Anna wasn't as happy about the prospect of seeing Philip again, but it was something she had to do. As Aunt Beth had written, a final meeting might allow Anna to dismiss him from her mind even if it achieved little else. What had concerned Anna, though, was Aunt Beth saying that Philip didn't know she was to be one of the party.

What must he think of her if Aunt Beth thought that her presence might keep him away?

"Do you wish for some refreshment, my lady?" the maid

4

asked, as Anna emerged from the small room set aside for ladies' use.

Anna hesitated. The groom had said they were only an hour from Beechgrove, but it hardly seemed fair to the inn to leave without buying something.

"The private parlour's occupied, my lady, but it's only a gentleman. I'm sure he won't mind sharing. Captain Kempton, it is. He's known in these parts, so you needn't worry."

Philip? Here?

Her heart fluttered—she had not expected to see him so soon.

It shouldn't be so surprising; they were both on their way to the same place, after all. But although it was a fortnight since she'd received Aunt Beth's letter, she still had not decided what she should say to him. She'd thought she would have a little more time to consider, but perhaps a first meeting here would be best. If he ignored her or just walked away, there would be no witnesses.

"A glass of wine, if you please."

Anna took a deep breath. She had until the maid returned to compose herself. She smoothed her skirts—she looked smart enough. Knowing she was dressed well helped to stoke her confidence.

It wasn't the maid who returned, but the landlord, with a glass of wine on a small tray. "This way, my lady."

Anna followed him down the dimly lit passage, hesitating by the parlour door as the landlord entered.

"There's a lady here, Captain. I hoped you won't mind her sharing the parlour while she drinks her wine."

The landlord blocked her view of the room.

"By all means."

Anna's breath caught. The sound of his voice was still familiar after all this time, and her hands clenched until the nails bit into her palms. Then the landlord moved into the room to set her wine on an empty table, and she was looking directly at Philip.

He'd changed, and he hadn't. The same hazel eyes, but with more creases at their corners. The same brown hair, a little lighter than she remembered, perhaps bleached by the tropical sun. The smile was cool, a smile for a stranger.

Had he forgotten her so completely? Was that why he'd never answered her letters?

Philip saw only a dark red pelisse beyond the landlord as he agreed to share the parlour. He hadn't paid for the privilege of having it to himself, after all. As he stood, the woman's face came into view and his polite smile froze.

How could *she* be here?

For a moment he wondered if his thoughts had conjured up a vision, then she moved and the spell was broken.

"Captain Kempton." She inclined her head and turned to the landlord. "Thank you. Can you ask my groom to be ready in ten minutes?"

The landlord bowed and left, leaving the door ajar. Anna, his Anna, sat down at the table and sipped her wine. He dragged his eyes away from her face, dismayed to find he was still attracted to her in spite of what she had done.

'Please, Captain, do finish your meal."

Her voice sounded different than it did in his dreams—cooler, more confident. He sat down but ignored the food. "You look well, Anna. My lady, I should say." What was her name now? He'd destroyed the letter—all he could remember was that the man had a title.

"I am Lady Radnor now," she said. "You seem to be none the worse for your sojourn in the tropics, Captain. I should congratulate you on being made post."

"And I should congratulate you on your marriage."

Despite his efforts, bitterness coloured his tone. She had done well for herself; he could see that from her garments. Edgings and trim of deep pink turned what might have been a drab pelisse into one of understated elegance, an effect that was unlikely to have come cheap. Her hair was dressed plainly, as it had been that summer, twisted into a knot with only a few tendrils to frame her face.

"Thank you. But my husband died two years ago."

"Commiserations, my lady." He tried to sound sincere, and was ashamed of himself for the effort it took.

"It was not unexpected," she said, a shadow crossing her face. "But it is always sad when a good man dies."

Good man? Taking a wife young enough to have been his granddaughter?

Anna—Lady Radnor—drank more of her wine, her fingers cradling the glass. He wanted to reach out and touch them, to caress her cheek, feel if her skin was as smooth as before. She had more poise now than when they first met, but to his dismay the new maturity this gave her only added to the need filling him.

"I was sorry you did not reply to my letter, Captain. I wrote again, in case the first one did not reach you."

Philip felt the heat rise to his face.

"So either several letters went astray, or you decided not to reply." She paused for a moment. "Or perhaps you did not even read them."

He lowered his eyes, one hand toying with his knife. He had received a letter from her after he'd already learned of her marriage. He'd read only enough to realise who the letter was from, then held it in a candle flame, watching the paper char and burn until there was nothing left but ash. After what she had done, writing to him had seemed like an insult.

Her chair scraped on the floor as she stood. "Thank you

for allowing me to share the parlour. I bid you good day, Captain."

She left without waiting for an answer, although he had no idea what he could have said. He pushed the plate away and went to the window. A chaise stood ready. A groom put up the steps behind her and closed the door. It pulled away, taking the road to the north—the same way he was travelling.

Could she be going to Beechgrove too? She must be—why else would she be on this road, today?

The desire to turn back was stronger than ever, but so were the reasons to carry on. If he went home now, *she* would know he'd cried craven, as well as Aunt Beth and any others who remembered that summer house party.

His legs and backside protested as he finally pulled himself up into the saddle, having drunk perhaps one mug of mulled ale too many. It was just as well the way from here had few turnings.

In no rush to arrive, he let the horse amble on through a landscape of black shadows and silhouettes, the only sounds the clop of the horse's hooves on stone and frozen mud. The cold was no worse than many a night at sea in the Channel, and here, at least, he was dry.

He'd last ridden this road four years ago, on a sunny July afternoon. Aunt Beth had greeted him and directed him to where her younger guests were picnicking beyond the woods on the lower slopes of Delfont Down. That was where he'd first met Anna.

He hadn't noticed her at first. Half a dozen adults sat on blankets spread on the grass, with as many children of varying ages chattering around them and poring over sheets of paper. His cousin Toby had risen as he approached, and clapped him on the shoulder in welcome. He recognised Thalia, Aunt Beth's younger daughter—she must be fifteen or so now. A quick glance showed that most of the others present were cousins on Aunt Beth's side of the family and their offspring—cousins he didn't know well.

A heap of sticks, string and spades lay nearby. Further up the slope, a few patches of white showed where someone had dug up the turf to reveal the chalk beneath. Mystified, Philip asked what they were doing.

"Designing a horse to go on the hillside," one of the boys piped up.

"Or a giant," another added, looking up from his drawing.

"Someone told them about schoolboys at Marlborough making a white horse on land near the town," Toby explained. "Mama said they could make one here, but they'd have to dig the turf out themselves." He nodded to the patches of white further up the hill. "They dug a couple of holes to check the chalk isn't too far down here."

"There is a recent figure at Weymouth, too, with King George on it." The woman who spoke had a soft voice, and grey eyes set in an oval face. A young girl sat on the blanket beside her, holding a sketch pad and pencil. "It was made about two years ago."

"And Uncle Toby has been telling us about the giant at Cerne."

Philip suppressed a smile. Uncle Thomas had a booklet about the chalk figures of England, and he and Toby had sniggered over the drawing of the giant when they were boys. The naked figure was... 'well endowed' might be a polite way of putting it. "How big is his weapon, Toby, can you remember?"

Toby smirked, resuming his recumbent position on the

blanket. "You read the same book as I did, Phil. You tell them."

The woman's lips compressed, as if she were suppressing a smile. She gazed up at Philip with wide, innocent eyes—too innocent. "His club, do you mean?" Her cheeks dimpled, and he felt a flush of embarrassment that she'd understood his indelicate allusion.

"Anna's been there," the first boy said. "She said we could go to see it when we're older. Uncle Edward says Emily mustn't—"

"Let the gentleman speak, James," Anna admonished, and the lad subsided.

"His club must be a hundred feet long, I think," Philip said. He made a bow. "Lieutenant Philip Kempton, at your service."

"Anna Tremayne." She smiled, those dimples appearing again. "These are my cousins, James and Emily." Both children had the same dark brown hair, but their faces bore little resemblance to hers. The boy looked to be around ten years old, the girl a little younger.

Miss or Mrs Tremayne, he wondered, then shook his head. It mattered not—he was here for only a few weeks.

"I don't think Aunt Beth would approve of a copy of the giant here," Philip said.

"Why not?" James asked.

"I..." Too late, Philip realised the impossibility of explaining why not in front of young girls and women.

Anna Tremayne watched him with interest as he foundered for words, then one corner of her mouth curved upwards before she turned to her cousin.

"Well, James, if his club is a hundred feet long, he must be about twice as tall as that. How long do you think it would take you boys to cut lines in the grass to make a giant that big?"

"We could have a smaller giant," another boy suggested.

"Remember Aunt Beth said you had to dig the figure yourselves?" Anna said. "You could only make a very small giant, then he wouldn't be a giant at all."

The boys' faces fell.

"You could have a horse, or a dog," Philip suggested, relieved to be let off the hook.

"Horses are too common," one of the boys objected. "We want ours to be different."

"What kind of dog? Like Aunt Beth's spaniel?" James could hardly have shown less enthusiasm.

"Cerberus, perhaps?" Anna suggested.

James' brow creased in thought, before he dredged the knowledge from his memory. "The dog that guards the underworld—"

"With three heads!" the other lad added.

"You could ask Emily to draw it for you," Anna suggested.

"Then it will be time for the picnic," one of the other women announced.

Philip wandered away; Toby got to his feet and followed him. Wildflowers grew amongst the grass, and Philip bent to pick purple scabious and knapweed, white umbels of wild carrot and trembling harebells. These were some of the things he missed while at sea.

"Who is Miss Tremayne?" he asked.

"Daughter of Mama's best friend from her schooldays," Toby said. "The friend died some years ago, though, and Anna lives with her uncle and those two children. Mama invites Anna quite often—I'm surprised you've never met her."

He hadn't—he would have remembered. In repose, her face was pleasing: a clear skin, touched by the summer sun, a mouth that looked as if it smiled a lot. The way she'd laughed at him before coming to his aid had been entrancing.

She was not married—Toby had not contradicted his use of 'Miss'.

"Wooing her with flowers?" Toby asked.

"Thanking her, rather."

"Ha! That served you right for trying to embarrass me."

But, looking back, the flowers *had* been the first stage in courting her; that had become plain soon enough. He'd thought the attraction that had grown during those weeks— love, even—had faded, but their brief meeting at the inn had been sufficient to show he'd been mistaken. His want for her was as strong as ever, despite her betrayal.

He wrenched his mind away from his memories, gazing up at the infinity of stars. Ursa Minor hung above the lane he rode, guiding his way north. He turned his thoughts to the decision he had to make soon. What was he going to do with himself now the war was over? The *Penelope* had already been broken up—she'd been old and timeworn before he'd been given command. With no ship, and a surfeit of officers on half-pay, it was time he gave serious consideration to what he would do with the rest of his life.

If he had to avoid Anna—Lady Radnor—while he was at Beechgrove, perhaps that would give him time to consider Admiral Lord Harpenden's suggestion.

CHAPTER 2

*A*nna clasped her hands inside her muff as the chaise moved off, dismayed to find they were shaking. It had been more than four years since she'd seen him, and over three since she'd given up hope that he would reply to her letter. She should not be having this reaction.

Thank goodness she'd stopped at the inn—now, at least, she had some time in the chaise to try to regain her calm.

What had he thought of her? She could not tell. His cool, initial, smile had indeed been for a stranger, but when he'd recognised her his face had become unreadable, blank. The faint hope of his being pleased to see her had vanished.

The way he'd avoided her eyes when she wondered if he had read her letters had been telling—she guessed he had received them but had not looked at her explanation. If he'd cared for her, why wouldn't he have read them?

If he felt nothing for her, why hadn't he just said so?

She rested her head against the squabs. It was going to be difficult to maintain a cheerful front for the few days she would be at Beechgrove, but she must do her best. It might be too late to mend the misunderstandings between them, but she would at least like to know if he had meant those words of love when he'd said them.

Anna's spirits lifted as the carriage turned into the drive. Although the house was just a black shadow against the starry sky, she'd visited it so often that she could see it in her mind. Originally a small Jacobean manor, Beechgrove had been extended by different owners and was now a hodge-podge of different styles. No one could call it elegant, but it looked comfortable, settled in its surrounding gardens and woodland at the foot of a grassy hillside.

As she hurried up the steps the front door opened, spilling light into the dark. Aunt Beth stood in the doorway, the usual wisps of greying hair escaping their pins.

"Welcome, my dear!" Beth gave Anna a quick hug and a peck on the cheek, and drew her into the hall. "It seems an age since I've seen you!"

"Less than six months." Anna removed her bonnet and gloves. "But yes—too long. It is good to be here." Apart from her young cousins, the Kemptons were the nearest thing she had to family, and it was comforting to be with them over Christmastide. "You should come to Weymouth more often, Beth. There is plenty of room to put you up."

"Perhaps I will, but only when James is away at school." Beth shook her head. "I find I'm getting too old to keep up with energetic schoolboys, even though you've brought James up to be well-mannered. My brood are here for the whole twelve days; luckily the grandchildren are still young enough to be confined to the nursery most of the time. But come in and warm yourself. Bates will have your trunk taken to your room."

The parlour was light and cheerful, the cream coloured wallpaper and yellow upholstery reflecting the lamplight. Books and papers strewn across a table near the window showed recent occupation.

"They're all dressing for dinner," Beth explained as Anna crossed to the blazing fire and held her hands to its warmth. "What have you done with James and Emily? Your note said only that you would be coming alone."

"I thought it best under the circumstances. They were both invited to spend a few days with school friends, but I do need to return the day after Boxing Day. I had hoped to be here earlier, but it took longer to see them off than I'd thought." Her hands now fully thawed, she took a seat near Beth.

"As is always the way with children. It is a pity you could not stay longer. Perhaps they could come here instead for the last days of Christmas?"

"No, not with Philip—" Anna took a deep breath. "I stopped at the Blue Bell on the way. I met Captain Kempton there. He…" She swallowed.

Beth leaned over and patted her knee. "No need to tell me if you do not wish to, my dear. I hope it was not a mistake to invite the two of you. I'm afraid it is to be only a small party for Christmastide. Apart from my children and their families, Philip is the only other guest."

Anna tried to maintain her polite smile, but Aunt Beth was too perceptive.

"Don't worry about being forced together, Anna. I have lots of activities planned. There will be no need to be paired off into couples, and no need to participate at all unless you wish to. Now, do you need to change for dinner, or would you prefer a tray in your room for this evening? If so, I'll look in on you after dinner and you can tell me what James and Emily have been up to. I'll not have you brooding alone *all* evening."

"I'd be happy to have a tray, thank you." Philip could arrive at any moment, and she didn't want to face him again in front of the whole Kempton family. Not yet.

. . .

Aunt Beth left Anna alone after their exchange of family news. Now she could either spend a dull evening alone in her room or she could venture downstairs and explain that she'd missed dinner because she'd been tired from her journey. Talking to Beth's children and their spouses would take her mind off her memories, but she would also be likely to encounter Philip. He must have arrived by now, unless he had changed his mind about coming. Would he take the coward's way out to avoid her?

That thought decided her. What was she doing but behaving like a coward herself? Downstairs, she would be able to get used to seeing him in company without having to talk to him directly.

Inspecting the evening gowns she had brought with her, she chose a simple one in cream satin with a yellow sash and small knots of matching ribbon around the hem. She looked well in it, but no one would assume she had dressed to impress. It didn't take her long to arrange the usual simple knot in her hair.

Fate was against her, it seemed. As she reached the foot of the stairs a knock sounded on the front door, and Bates opened it.

"Welcome, Captain. You are later than we expected—have you had some mishap?"

Encountering Philip alone in the hall was not what she had in mind.

"No, Bates. I merely…" The rest of Philip's words faded as she slipped into Uncle Thomas' small library and closed the door behind her.

The room was empty, only the flickering light from the fire illuminating the bookcases and furniture. This was a quiet retreat for anyone who found the hubbub of Kempton life fatiguing. That was often the case at Beechgrove, with many cousins on both sides of the family welcome to visit whenever it took their fancy.

It had been a retreat for her four years ago, too. Although Anna loved her little cousins dearly, the chance to leave them playing with the other youngsters had been a welcome relief at times. Lieutenant Kempton, understandably, had also wanted to escape, and she'd found him in here the first evening of his stay. They had been in this room together several times after that, but one time in particular stood out in her memory.

They had enjoyed several days of sunshine, a time in which Lieutenant Kempton had enthusiastically joined the two boys in the creation of the chalk Cerberus, leaving her free to lounge on a blanket nearby and read a novel while Emily and Thalia sketched. And the lieutenant had helped her to organise the ceremonial unveiling when the thing was finished.

Then the weather turned. A day of patchy drizzle still allowed the houseful of children to release some of their energy in the gardens, and the adults had amused themselves acting selected scenes from Shakespeare. But when the following morning dawned too wet for anyone to wish to be out of doors most of the menfolk cravenly retreated to the Delfont Arms, leaving their wives to keep the children entertained. Lieutenant Kempton, for reasons unknown to her, had opted to stay, and soon a game of hide and go seek was suggested. Thalia, the younger Kempton daughter, declared the entertainment childish and retreated to her room with a book, while Aunt Beth declared she needed to consult the housekeeper.

James was delighted to draw the short straw as the first seeker.

"Do you want me to come with you?" Anna asked Emily.

Emily shook her head, her dark ringlets bobbing. "I'm eight now," she protested. "I can hide by myself!"

Anna tried not to laugh. "So you can. Very well then. Mary is but five, do you think I should help her instead?"

"Oh, yes. Five is only little." Emily laughed and ran off as Mary's mother mouthed her thanks, taking the hand of her even younger son.

"I'm counting up to fifty!" James called, his hands over his eyes. "One, two, three…"

The hall full of people emptied.

"James, don't find the young ones first," Anna whispered. "Let them think they're hidden well."

James nodded without removing his hands. "…fifteen, sixteen, seventeen…"

Anna hadn't seen which directions the others had taken. Mary would still be climbing the stairs when James finished counting, so they had to conceal themselves somewhere on this floor.

"…twenty-nine, thirty, thirty-one…"

Uncle Thomas' library was close. The door stood slightly ajar, and Anna led Mary in, a finger to her lips.

Perhaps this was not a good choice after all, Anna thought. A desk stood in one corner, there was a cloth-covered table near the window, and a couple of armchairs were arranged either side of the fire.

The table it would have to be. Mary giggled as Anna tip-toed exaggeratedly towards the table, then shrieked as a hand appeared at the bottom of the cloth and lifted it up.

"Sshhh," Anna whispered, her own heart racing with the surprise.

"Coming!" James' shout echoed in the hallway.

The hand beckoned. "Hurry up!" Lieutenant Kempton's head popped out. "He'll find you if you don't hide."

Mary scurried under the table, but Anna hesitated. She could just sit and pretend to read; after all, she was helping Mary, not playing the game herself.

"Come on, Anna!" Mary whispered. "Please!"

Anna sighed and crawled under the cloth, sitting with her knees drawn up under the centre of the table. It was not a large space, but at least the legs were at the corners so they all fitted—just. Not much of the day's grey light made its way through the cloth, but she could make out the lieutenant's smile.

"Welcome to my lair, Miss Tremayne," he said, his sepulchral tone belied by the laughter in his expression.

Beside her, Mary giggled, then the three of them sat still with only the sound of their breathing breaking the silence. The air held a hint of lemon and spices mingled with the lavender water she was wearing—his cologne? Anna felt strangely breathless, her pulse still beating fast and a strange feeling in her stomach. How ridiculous to feel that way about a game of hide and go seek.

"Found you!"

Mary grabbed Anna's arm as they heard James' call, even though he was not in the library. The little hand gripped tighter as footsteps sounded.

"Someone's bound to be in here—come on." James must have joined forces with the first hider he'd found.

"We're about to be discovered, I think," Lieutenant Kempton whispered. "What do you say to giving young James a scare?"

Mary's giggle was sufficient answer. The lieutenant leaned against Anna in the tight space as he brought his feet up under him, lifting the edge of the tablecloth with one hand. In the extra light, she could see the grin on his face.

"There's no one under the desk."

The footsteps came closer, and the lieutenant's thigh brushed against her arm as he leapt out with a roar. Mary's hand tightened on hers at the sudden movement, then she giggled as the two boys shrieked.

"That frightened them," Anna said to Mary, crawling out after her. The lieutenant held a hand out to help her up, his shoulders shaking with laughter.

She got to her feet, his hand warm on hers, and brushed dust from her gown. The two boys were convulsed with laughter; Lieutenant Kempton just stood there with a grin on his face.

"I've still found you, sir," James gasped.

"So you have. Why don't you take Mary along to help look for the others?"

The nervous fluttering of her heart had not abated; the look in his eyes as they met hers made her breath catch. She'd never felt this way before, but she knew it was nothing to do with the childish game.

"Yes, that's a good idea," she said, not looking at her cousin.

"Come on, Mary." James took the girl's hand and the boys led her out of the room. "Let's look in the billiards room."

"How old are you, lieutenant?" she asked, pleased that her voice sounded fairly normal.

He smiled down at her. "Oh, I don't know. About ten?"

She laughed, and the odd feelings turned into a warm glow.

"Please, won't you call me Philip?"

She felt her cheeks warm, although there was no reason why she shouldn't. She was not related to the Kemptons, but she'd been calling Toby by his Christian name for years as if he really were a cousin. Why should doing the same with this man feel different?

"Very well, Philip." It felt right, somehow, to call him that. "What do you intend to do now you have excused us from the game?"

"I think those lads should have cleared the billiards room by now. Do you play?"

Recalling that day now, Anna wrapped her arms around herself in the warm glow of the fire. They'd spent some time in the billiards room, most of it with the table between them. The feelings his presence induced had been interesting—enjoyable, even—but she'd been wary of encouraging them too quickly.

She'd soundly beaten him, having spent many a wet day at Beechgrove playing with Toby, and with Lizzie too. Back then Thalia had been too young to wield a cue. Philip had taken it in good part, claiming the inability to practise while at sea as his excuse.

Aunt Beth had said all her children had come for Christmas. They would be here somewhere, together with the spouses of the older two. It was time for her to stop hiding and go to greet the company.

∾

"The ladies are in the parlour, sir," Bates said as he closed the front door behind Philip and took his hat and gloves. "The gentlemen are still with their port in the dining room. Your room is ready if you wish to change, and cook can provide a meal if you require it."

"No, thank you, Bates. I ate on the way." Guiltily conscious of the time he'd spent at the Blue Bell after Anna had left, Philip shed his coat and handed it to the butler. Aunt Beth had probably been expecting him for dinner.

He looked down at his clothing. Although the dry, cold weather meant he didn't have the usual spattering of mud on his breeches and boots, his clothing still bore the marks of travel. Joining the ladies was out of the question unless he changed, but Uncle Thomas and his cousins wouldn't mind. That was just an excuse, though, he admitted to himself.

"The dining room, I think, but I don't need food."

The butler handed Philip's garments to a footman and opened the dining room door. "Captain Kempton."

"Philip!" Toby called, getting to his feet. "We expected you long since—is all well?"

"Yes." Philip forced a smile. "It's good to be here. Uncle Thomas. Anthony."

"It must be six years since we've seen you, Philip," Anthony said. "Since I wed Lizzie?"

"Indeed." He remembered cousin Lizzie's wedding, a couple of years before he'd met Anna, but he'd been at sea when Toby married Catherine. "How are things with you?" He pulled out a chair and sat down, accepting a glass of port. His mother and sisters had written long letters full of family news over the years, but he welcomed any opportunity to avoid the reason for his late arrival.

'Where's everyone else?" he asked, when the recitals of family history came to an end.

"You're the last," Uncle Thomas said. "There's only these two, with their wives and brats, and Thalia, of course. And Anna arrived a couple of hours ago—you've met Anna, haven't you? Anna Tremayne, as was."

"Of course he has, father. Anna was here when Phil came on leave before going off to the Caribbean."

"Yes, I remember Anna." There was no knowing look from Toby—if he'd worn his heart too much on his sleeve that summer, at least his cousin and uncle didn't appear to remember. Cousin Lizzie, likely to be more observant about such things, had been visiting friends then. He'd been expecting a much larger party. With so few guests, he'd find it difficult to keep his feelings hidden and avoid Anna.

Was Aunt Beth trying to throw them together?

Unless... What if Anna wasn't the reason he'd been invited?

"Is Thalia not wed yet?" She must be old enough now. All he remembered was a pretty girl who seemed to always be attaching herself to the adults in the party rather than playing with the children. Not that he could blame her for that—what girl of that age wanted to spend time with cousins still in the nursery?

"She spent some time in Town this spring," Toby said. "I gather she had a few offers, but rejected them all. Some nonsense about her heart already being given. Catherine was increasing at the time, so we weren't there. Thalia's to go again next year."

"That'll be her last chance in London," Uncle Thomas muttered. "Too expensive."

"But that's women's stuff, Phil," Toby added. "Tell us about that action off Guadalupe. The papers never give enough detail on such things."

Quite willing to spin out his time away from Aunt Beth's probable questions, Philip moved the dishes of cheese and sweetmeats around to represent islands, and pressed glasses and knives into service as frigates. He could make this story last for some time, then claim he was tired from his long ride.

"We had good luck in our sailing master," he started. "Knew all the shoals and reefs..."

CHAPTER 3

*P*hilip did not wake until first light the following morning, in spite of the turmoil of his thoughts. He threw back the covers and went to the window. The sky was clear, a few stars still visible as black turned to grey. A pale line on the south-eastern horizon showed where the sun would rise. It would be cold out, but perhaps a walk would help to loosen the sore muscles in his legs and backside. And perhaps also help him think what he would say to Anna, for he couldn't avoid meeting her today.

He dressed in the clothes he'd arrived in, leaving his clean sets for Uncle Thomas' valet to press. A couple of maids were about in the corridors, carrying scuttles of coal to set fires in the bedrooms. He told one not to bother with his room, and made his way to the kitchens. He'd stayed here often as a child, and important details of the house—such as where to wheedle food from Cook—had stuck in his memory.

With a cup of coffee inside him, he set off through the gardens. At sea, dawn had always been one of his favourite times, a period of calm before the routines of the day began. Now he crossed the lawns, frosted grass crisp beneath his boots and his breath making puffs of mist in the still air. Beyond the hedge was a small belt of woodland, bare branches stark against the lightening sky, and then he was on the grassy slope of the downs. He pushed himself hard until he reached the top, then paused to take in the view stretching around him.

He stood and watched the rising sun turn the sky to pastel blue. He'd walked up here with Anna several times during that summer fortnight—sometimes with others, later just the two of them. Now, as always, he enjoyed the beauty of the changing colours, but he couldn't help thinking that it would be even better with Anna beside him. The Anna he'd fallen in love with.

Freezing fingers and toes finally forced him to move. He made his way down by a different route, heading for the place where the chalk dog had been.

It was still there, the white lines sharp against the grass— someone must have weeded the gaps in the turf a few times since it was created. He'd initially helped with the making of it as an excuse to be near Anna as she kept an eye on her young cousins, but he'd been surprised to find he enjoyed working with the boys. Was it because he'd stayed here so often as a youth that he reverted so easily to enjoying children's games?

That had been the first time he'd seriously contemplated what it might be like to have children of his own. The idea of a family had become more concrete, rather than merely a vague expectation. Had he sensed, even in those first few days, that Anna might be a woman he could enjoy being with for the rest of his life?

He set off back to the house. Above, long wisps of high cloud were drifting in from the west. Perhaps there was snow on the way.

~

Ready to help Aunt Beth with preparations inside the house, Anna was surprised when Lizzie appeared and handed her a basket and a large pair of scissors. "Catherine's staying in, so I need you to come and gather holly, ivy, and mistletoe. Thalia will be along in a minute, and Anthony."

"Our official tree-climber?"

"Indeed." Lizzie laughed. "He likes the excuse to behave like a schoolboy now and then. The others have gone out to look for a Yule log."

Anna liked Lizzie and her husband—both had easy-going personalities with a sense of fun. Anna suspected that Lizzie would turn out very like her mother, with Beth's liking for being surrounded with friends and family. She'd probably turn plump like Beth, too, with her fondness for sweetmeats, but plumpness seemed to suit the Kempton women.

Anthony had joined Lizzie by the time Anna returned in her pelisse and half boots, Thalia trailing behind her down the stairs. Since she reached an age to attend balls and assemblies, Thalia had become more particular about her clothing than her sister had ever been. Today she wore a pale green pelisse trimmed with white fur around the neck. A matching bonnet and a huge fur muff completed the ensemble.

"Very practical, Thalia!" Lizzie said. "Are you sure you want to wear that? You're bound to get mud on it."

"It's a stupid idea to send me out for ivy." Thalia's pretty mouth pursed in what could only be called a scowl. "There are plenty of servants to do it."

"The fun is in finding it ourselves," Lizzie said. She picked up her own basket and shears and led the way across the gardens. Anna didn't comment, wondering at the change in the girl. She had never been particularly friendly towards

Anna, but this morning at breakfast she had been almost rude.

The narrow belt of trees behind the house widened to the east, and Uncle Thomas' gardeners kept the paths free of brambles and nettles. The frost had not reached far into the wood, and the paths were indeed soft with mud. Lizzie and Anna wandered happily along, inspecting the closer trees for the greenery they were seeking.

Anna pointed to an ancient trunk sheathed in ivy. "Here's a good one."

"Anthony, come and employ your stick on these brambles," Lizzie called. They stood back while Anthony set to with a will. Anna approached the tree, carefully holding in her pelisse to keep it away from the thorns on the battered stems. She began to pull on the strands of ivy, prising them away from the trunk with her scissors, cutting off lengths and passing them to Lizzie.

"I'm bored," Thalia muttered. "And cold. My nose is turning red."

"Well, walk on and look for mistletoe," Lizzie suggested. "Or holly. Anna, can you reach that long piece just above you?"

"It's too muddy," Thalia whined.

"Oh, for heaven's sake, Thalia!" Lizzie exclaimed. "Take your long face back to the house if you don't want to be here."

"I can't go by myself."

"You've been playing in these woods—"

"Allow me to escort you, Thalia," Anthony interrupted. "It would be a shame to dirty such a beautiful garment, especially when it suits you so well."

Thalia hesitated, then laid a hand on his bent arm. Anna suppressed a smile as Lizzie shook her head, and chuckled aloud as the departing Anthony grimaced over his shoulder.

"I'm sorry, Anna. I don't know what's got into her. Now, have we taken all we can from that tree?"

"I think so." Anna made her way back to the path. They would have to harvest what they could from trees that didn't need Anthony's assistance to get through the surrounding brambles.

Philip, having managed to avoid the breakfast room while the women were present, was relieved to find that Anna would be helping Aunt Beth in the house, while the men of the family were to locate and bring home a Yule log.

"We'll look in the woods to the west," Uncle Thomas announced. "It'll take several hours to find something suitable, I'm sure," he added, as they entered the woods. "Small enough to fit our fireplace, but big enough to stay alight for at least a few days." He paused at a log lying close to the path, tilted his head to one side, then strode on.

"What's wrong with that one?" Philip asked. Surely his uncle couldn't judge it too big by eye alone?

"Not a thing," Toby said with a laugh. "You've not been here at Christmas before, have you?"

Philip shook his head.

"We're heading for a few pints in the Delfont Arms. Father got the gardener to find that log weeks ago." He lowered his voice. "He thinks Mama doesn't know."

"Does she?"

"Of course. She prefers the men out from under her feet while she's making the final preparations."

"I say, wait a moment."

The call came from behind, and they all stopped and turned. Anthony waved at them, just visible through the bare trunks. He had a woman with him—not Anna, Philip was relieved to see. Thalia, now a pretty young woman. They waited while Anthony made his slow way towards them.

"Thalia, what are you doing here?" Uncle Thomas asked.

"I wanted to help find the Yule log, Papa," she said, casting a quick glance towards Philip as she spoke. "It's no fun cutting ivy with Lizzie."

"You said you wanted to return to the house to prevent your pelisse getting muddy." Anthony was clearly struggling to keep exasperation from his voice.

"This is just as muddy as the east woods," Uncle Thomas said. "Go back, Thalia."

Philip moved a few steps away, not wanting to witness a family argument.

"Come on, Thalia," Anthony said. "Lizzie'll have my head if I don't get back to help her."

"But I want to come with—"

"No, Thalia." Uncle Thomas was beginning to sound uncharacteristically curt. "I'll take you back." He turned to the rest of them. "I'll see you in the pub later."

Thalia pouted, but said nothing further. She looked at Philip again, a tentative smile on her lips.

"I'll escort her, Uncle," Philip offered, and Thalia's smile widened. "And, Anthony, I can give Lizzie a hand, if you wish." He didn't feel like drinking the day away, and Lizzie was always pleasant company.

"Thanks Philip. I owe you a favour."

The men trooped off, and Thalia smiled up at him as she took his arm.

"It is such a long time since I've seen you, Captain."

"Yes, indeed." What else could he say, particularly as she must have been the fourth or fifth person to say so since he arrived? "That happens when one is in the Navy."

"Papa read out the reports of your actions in the Gazette."

"That must have made for poor entertainment." Please, not the 'brave sailors' speech again.

"I do so admire the courageous men who fight for our country."

Philip grunted.

"Anna says you must have earned lots of prize money."

"Oh." The fact that Anna had thought about him enough to follow his career shouldn't lift his spirits.

"She must be looking for another rich husband by now," Thalia went on. "She's been out of mourning for nearly a year."

The lift to his spirits vanished. "You have had a season in London, I understand?" He was not going to discuss Anna with Thalia.

"Oh yes. I was a great success, and much admired."

He glanced at her as he spoke. Was she fluttering her eyelashes at him? Surely not. "You have a suitor, then?"

She gazed up at him, a coy smile on her lips. "Oh, no. I did have several offers, but I did not care for any of them."

Thalia *was* flirting with him. He increased his pace, hoping that the speed would not leave her enough breath to talk. Fortunately they soon emerged from the woods.

"Here we are," he said, unnecessarily. "I'm sure you can make your own way back across the gardens." He lifted her hand from his arm as he spoke. There was no need for him to escort her all the way to the house.

"I will come with you."

She reached out to take his arm again, but he clasped his hands behind his back. The expression that reduced errant midshipmen to quavering excuses didn't have quite the same effect on her, but she did take a step away.

"It will still be as muddy as it was when you left." Philip spoke firmly.

"I shan't mind if—"

"Excuse me." How transparent could she be? He strode off without waiting for a reply.

One advantage of being on active service had been the absence of marriage-minded females. He hadn't expected to find one here. At least Cousin Lizzie's chatter would be innocuous, and she was safely married. He wasn't sure exactly where to find her, but he was not going to go back and ask Thalia for directions.

He headed for the east woods. Once in the trees he chose a path at random and slowed his pace. Flattened brambles and a criss-cross pattern in the mud where someone had set down a basket indicated that he was going the right way. Finally, he heard a murmur of voices. Lizzie must be with Toby's wife.

Or Anna—that sounded like Anna's voice.

He stopped, but he was too late; Lizzie had heard his approach. "Anthony? Come and help! You've been an age!"

He had no choice but to join them. Lizzie stood alone beneath a tree, pulling strands of ivy from its trunk. A basket of the stuff rested on the path nearby. She turned her head as he trod through the undergrowth.

"Anthony went with the others to the Delfont Arms."

"Typical!" Lizzie shook her head. "Still, he did escort Thalia back for us."

"It's no use, Lizzie, we'll have to wait until— Oh!" Anna rounded a bend in the path ahead, coming to an abrupt halt as she saw him. "Captain Kempton." She nodded briefly; nothing in her expression said she was pleased to see him.

"Lady Radnor," he said. Cold or exertion had reddened her face, but did nothing to reduce the attraction he felt.

Lizzie's gaze flicked from Anna to himself and back again. "Oh, don't be so stuffy, you two. Phil, Anna was trying to reach some mistletoe, but neither of us are tall enough." She held out a pair of scissors. "Show him the way, Anna."

He pocketed the scissors and followed Anna along the path. She turned, walking a little way into the undergrowth, and pointed to a ball of mistletoe clinging to a thick branch above her head.

It was too far for him to reach, despite his greater height. "How did you think you could reach that?" Off balance at finding her here, his words came out harshly.

Her lips turned down at the corners for a second, then she shrugged. "I tried to climb up, but the branches are too far apart. At least, for someone wearing a dress."

"Allow me," he said, trying to dismiss an image of her wearing breeches to attempt the task. Jumping to get his hands around the branch, he pulled himself up until he could get one leg over it.

"Oh, very impressive, Phil!" Lizzie clapped, and he felt his face redden. He could easily have climbed up using stumps of old branches but no, he had to show off by doing it the hard way.

"Just cut off some pieces," his cousin ordered. "We don't need the whole thing. Throw them down."

He did as she said, and waited until the two women had gathered them up and returned to the path before letting himself down.

As he reached the path himself, Lizzie disappeared around a bend with a basket on each arm.

'You sent her back?" Philip asked, wondering if Anna was about to behave like Thalia.

Her lips compressed, and her eyes met his briefly before she looked away again. "No, I did not. She just said the baskets were full and she'd be back soon."

"Ah, I see." Her expression was far from flirtatious and, irrationally, he felt a slight pang of regret. "I was surprised to find you here at Beechgrove. Why have you come?"

"I was invited." Her chin lifted. "But if I had known my

presence would be so distasteful to you, I would not have accepted the invitation."

It wasn't what she said, but what she hadn't that made him pause. "Did you know I would be here?" Was Thalia right?

"Yes. Aunt Beth—"

"You thought a Captain with prize money might do now you are free to find another rich husband? One, this time, less than twice your age."

Her body stiffened. The hurt in her expression showed his assumption about her motive was wrong, but it was too late to unsay the words.

"You are mistaken, Captain. My late husband was at least three times my age." There was a faint tremor to her voice. "I came because I hoped to get a chance to explain why I married when I had promised to wait for you."

"Anna, I didn't—"

"But there seems little point," she went on. "I think we do not know each other as well as we once supposed. Good day, Captain Kempton."

She turned and stalked away.

CHAPTER 4

*A*nna took deep breaths as she walked, clenching her fists. She would not cry; the time for that had long gone. It was foolish to have come here, raking up past emotions, past hopes.

He'd assumed that she'd married only for money, and that she now wanted more. That breaking her promise had been easy. And he'd not even read her letter when she'd tried to explain.

She had believed he'd loved and respected her. And no matter what he did or didn't feel for her, she hadn't thought he was a man to leap to hasty judgements.

The path forked, and she turned away from the house, heading north out of the woods and onto the rising grass-land. Thin clouds veiled the sky, the sun showing through only as a white disc. The pale light leached colour from the landscape, matching her mood as she climbed.

She was trapped here for the next few days—she could not ask Beth to lend her the chaise again at this busy time. All she could do was to stay away from Philip as much as possible.

Reaching the rounded ridge, she turned east. She'd walked this way several times with Philip, usually with James running around them and Emily looking for flowers. On other visits to Beechgrove she'd come here with Lizzie and Anthony when they were courting, and occasionally with Aunt Beth and Uncle Thomas. Beth would wonder why she wasn't back at the house helping to arrange the evergreens she and Lizzie had gathered.

Let Philip explain, she thought. Aunt Beth would guess their meeting hadn't gone well.

Half an hour later, when she set off down the hill to loop through the fields and back to Beechgrove, she realised she'd made a mistake coming this way. There were too many memories up here. Watching as Philip helped James to fly his kite, both of them dashing up and down on the grass. Philip —surprisingly—telling Emily the names of all the flowers she'd collected and helping her to draw them. Amongst it all, little touches and exchanged glances, the warmth of his hand on the small of her back, the support of his arm when crossing rough ground, shared enjoyment of the glorious weather and the countryside.

Well, he'd given up on her quickly enough. He hadn't written, even before the events that led to her hasty marriage. She tried to stoke her anger against him as she strode on, but it didn't come. Instead, she felt regret for things that might have been, and a deep loneliness. Nothing had changed, really, with today's confrontation; it had merely reinforced the feeling that everything was over between them.

Her return route took her through the woods, and brought back the most vivid memory of all. She was *not* going to look for the clearing with a stream running through it. It would be too painful to see the last place they'd been together that summer.

. . .

Philip had come to her as she was helping Beth to cut flowers for the house, snipping dahlias and phlox, long stems of delphiniums and veronica.

"Walk with me?" he asked, his usual smile absent.

Anna hesitated, but Beth flapped a hand at her. "Go. I can manage this."

Philip had led her into the woods, arm in arm as had become their custom. The bubble of happiness that had been inside her for days began to evaporate as she took in the way his lips were pressed together.

"Daniels has just brought the post," he said.

"Orders?" What else would have removed the smile from his face?

"I'm afraid so. I'm wanted in Portsmouth immediately."

"Oh." She looked away, swallowing hard against a lump in her throat. "I thought you had another week." Even that had not seemed long enough.

"So did I, but it appears the *Garnet*'s first lieutenant has been taken ill, so I'm needed to supervise loading stores. I must leave this afternoon."

"That is a shame. I will miss our walks together." And the warm feeling when they were in contact as they were now. Without intending to, she found herself walking closer, so their arms touched as well. He put his hand on hers, where it rested on his arm, and gave a gentle squeeze.

"I will miss you too." There was sincerity in his deep voice.

They walked on in silence, still close, until they came to the glade. The stream burbled in the dappled shade, the cool air welcome after the sunshine in the gardens.

"Anna."

She turned to face him.

"Anna, I've never talked with a woman as I have with you here. Never shared my thoughts and wishes."

He raised his hand, as if he were about to touch her cheek, but let it drop again.

"I could be away for two years, or even longer. I don't think I'm giving away any secrets by telling you we're bound for the Caribbean. That's better than the East Indies, I suppose. Not quite as far away."

"So long?" She'd known he would have to go to sea, of course, but hadn't thought it would be so soon and for such a time. Or that the news would produce this hollow pit in her stomach. "I wish you well, Philip." She wanted to say more, but suddenly wondered if the time they'd spent together was just Philip's way of passing his leave pleasantly.

"Anna, we have only known each other a fortnight." He looked away, rubbing one hand through his hair.

It seemed as if she'd known him forever, the way they talked easily about everything and nothing, yet the feeling that had been growing inside her was something new. A heady emotion she'd thought she was going to have a little more time to explore.

"Anna..."

She waited, but rather than speaking he reached up and tugged gently on the ribbons beneath her chin, slowly pulling the bow loose. She could have stopped him had she wished to, but as her heart began to race she knew she did not. The knot fell undone, and she reached up and removed her bonnet, laying it on the grass.

"That's better," he said, his voice so quiet it was almost a whisper. He ran his fingers down her cheek and her breath caught as she raised her eyes to his. He took a step closer, until their bodies were almost touching. No man had stood close to her in this way before, but it felt right. Then he bent his head until their lips touched.

. . .

Anna put a hand to her cold face, recalling the heat of his mouth on hers, the thrill that shot right down to her toes as her lips parted and their tongues met.

She still wanted him, wanted to discover what came next. What it felt like to touch a man's bare flesh and have him touch her. How it felt to have the final joining. And with him —not with anyone else.

Mama had explained what happened in a marriage when Anna turned seventeen, just before her final illness. At the time, Anna had thought it sounded most unpleasant, but there had been a wistful look in Mama's eyes that told her there was more to it than a simple joining of bodies.

"Wait for me?" Philip had asked, when the kiss finally ended. She could still remember the sadness in his voice. "I should speak to your uncle before…" He gazed into her eyes. "There was so much we could have said, with only a little more time. Promise me you'll wait, Anna? Please?"

And she had promised.

Philip sat on a fallen log, gazing after Anna as she disappeared into the trees. What had possessed him to say such a thing? Thalia's suggestion had prompted it, but he hadn't really believed Anna would pursue him for his money. No, already irritated with himself for still wanting her, he'd lashed out with the most hurtful thing he could say.

Her words to him had hurt, too. They didn't know each other. There was no way in which he could twist that into something complimentary. She was disappointed in him. Yet it was *she* who had broken her promise.

The sound of female voices alerted him to Lizzie's return,

with company. He got to his feet and walked deeper into the woods, moving quietly. If Lizzie didn't spot him leaving, there would be no awkward questions later about why he was avoiding her.

He could loop around the house and make his way to the pub. The idea of drinking his sorrows away was beginning to seem more appealing, and the others would leave him in peace while he did so. But he would still have to face Aunt Beth and Anna later, and probably with a sore head.

Better just to walk. He wouldn't get lost while the rise of the downs behind the house showed his direction. Walk, and think.

He'd felt wronged for nearly four years. She'd promised to wait for him, and she hadn't.

The letter had reached him at a bad time.

He was leaning against the railing surrounding the quarter-deck of the *Garnet*, his hands gripping the wood to help him balance without putting weight on his injured leg. The graze caused by the flying splinter had stopped bleeding, but it hurt like the devil still.

He'd posted lookouts, but he scanned the horizon himself as well. It was unlikely there were any more enemy priva-teers this close to Antigua, but the ship couldn't survive another encounter. The captured vessel kept pace astern, now commanded by the *Garnet*'s third lieutenant.

In spite of his efforts not to dwell on the recent engage-ment, his every gaze over the far side of the ship paused on the row of canvas-wrapped bodies. One of the large ones was Gadstone, the first lieutenant and a good friend. The smaller bundles held the youngest midshipman and two of the powder monkeys.

So young.

The tree-clad hills above English Harbour loomed higher now; it would not be long before they could drop anchor. Thank God for that. He called to one of the seamen sweeping debris from the deck. "Leave that now, Tanner. Tell the captain we should be at anchor within the hour."

"Aye aye, sir." The man dashed off, down the companionway to where Captain Jerrick lay in his bunk. Informing him was merely a courtesy—with the loss of his leg, he was in no state to take charge.

You're turning soft, Philip told himself, glancing at those sad bundles of canvas again. He'd seen death at sea before—who had not? Perhaps it was that time he'd spent at Aunt Beth's last summer that made the loss of the youngest members of the crew so distressing. At that moment, he wanted nothing more than to be back on the sunlit downs, hand in hand with Anna. Hers was a different world—civilised, kind, happy. He allowed his mind to wander for a moment, imagining more—Anna in his arms, in his bed. Waking beside her each morning.

He was still on duty that evening as the sun neared the horizon, the *Garnet* safely moored in the shelter of Fort Berkeley. Three dockyard men were filling their notebooks with lists of repairs. The longboat, remarkably undamaged, was pulling towards them. The purser sat in the stern, having escorted the dead to the cemetery. They would be buried tomorrow.

He watched as Venner climbed aboard and mounted the steps to the quarterdeck.

"Got some post, sir."

"Very good. Hand it out when the men have dinner, if you please."

"Aye, sir. There's one for you." Venner took several letters from his satchel, sorting through them and picking one out.

Impatient, Philip held his hand out for it. Instead of just the single letter, Venner gave him several.

"The others are for Lieutenant Gadstone and Samuelson, sir."

Two of the canvas bundles the purser had taken ashore. Their correspondence would have to be returned to the senders, with an explanation.

"I'll deal with them," he said. It wasn't something he'd had to do before, but he'd helped Gadstone to write a few letters to next of kin. Now he'd have to do the same for Gadstone's wife.

He put those in his pocket as the purser left. A pang of disappointment struck as he examined the handwriting on the one addressed to him—it was not Anna's hand. Breaking the seal, he turned first to the signature. Aunt Beth.

Anna—married? The words *titled* and *rich* swam before his eyes. *Old enough to be her grandfather...so sorry to have to tell you...could not dissuade her.*

With an oath, he crumpled the letter and flung it over the side where it turned to pulp, tendrils of ink briefly visible as the words disappeared.

Philip picked at the bark on the log, remembering the days and weeks that had followed. He'd worked longer hours than he needed to, supervising the repair of the *Garnet.* Too much work was better than having too much time to think.

The woman who had become so precious to him had broken her word within a few months of giving it. And with the contents of that letter in mind, he'd destroyed hers without reading it when it arrived a few weeks later.

Had that been unfair? He hadn't thought so at the time, or even yesterday. What explanation could there be, after all? She'd chosen money and rank over a lowly naval lieutenant.

At least Aunt Beth had told him—better to know than to wait for letters from Anna that would never come.

Aunt Beth?

Although he couldn't remember the exact words of the letter, it had definitely been critical of Anna's choice. Almost spiteful, but that was not like his aunt. And Anna would not be here at Beechgrove without an invitation from Beth. Something must have made Beth change her mind.

He must apologise to Anna for his words today, and for his lack of faith, but perhaps he should talk to Beth first.

"It's about Anna," Philip started, as soon as he was alone in the library with his aunt. Beth sat in one of the worn leather armchairs by the fire, but he could not be still.

"Go on."

"Why did you invite her here?" he asked, pacing over to the window and back. "And why didn't you tell me?"

"Anna has a standing invitation to come here at any time she can get away. She spent last Christmas with us, although she brought her cousins then. I didn't tell you because I thought you might not come if you knew."

She was right. "Why did you want us to meet?"

"I thought it might help Anna's peace of mind if she could learn why you never responded to her letters. It might help you, too. Your mama writes that you have not been happy since you returned."

So his mother had conspired with Aunt Beth to get him here; that was why she'd been insistent that he accept the invitation. He ran a hand through his hair, wondering how much to tell Beth.

"I talked to Anna yesterday evening," Beth went on. "It must have been about the time you arrived. She thought you hadn't read the explanation she sent you."

Aunt Beth had kept any accusation from her voice, but Philip felt his face reddening again. "That is correct."

"Why?"

"Because of your letter."

"A letter from me? Philip, I don't write to you, any more than you do to me. Your mama lets you have all the news, and passes on what you tell her."

Aunt Beth hadn't written it? He felt his mind numb.

"Philip, what did the letter say?"

"That Anna had married only for title and rank."

Beth's eyes narrowed. "I can see how the fact of Anna's marriage could be presented in an uncomplimentary way, if the writer didn't know the reasons behind it. But I didn't write to you."

Philip gazed at her—there was no guile in his aunt's face, only puzzlement. If she hadn't written the letter, who had? He put that question to one side—mending things with Anna was more important at the moment.

"Philip?"

"The tone of the letter...the one that had your name on it..." He took a deep breath. "That was still in my mind when Anna's letter arrived. I didn't even open it."

Whoever *had* written it had poisoned his mind against a woman he'd loved—and still did, if the turmoil within him was any indication. And his own faith in her hadn't been strong enough to question it. He crossed to the window again, shame washing through him.

"What do you know about Anna's family?" Beth asked.

What had that to do with it?

"Philip? Do sit down, please. This may take a little time."

Obeying reluctantly, he sighed. "She was here with her young cousins, James and Emily," he recalled. "And she lives with their father, her uncle... Edward?"

Beth shook her head. "She did live with Edward, yes, but he never married."

Who were James and Emily, then? There had been so many other things to talk about at the time. Books and music, birds and flowers, art and history. It was Anna he had loved, and he liked her little cousins because she did.

"The Tremaynes had a lot of tragedy—I suppose she did not wish to dwell on such things," Beth said.

"I didn't give her chapter and verse on my own family, either."

"Well, it's time you knew something of her circumstances. Her father was the oldest of four children. He died when Anna was... around eleven, if I recall correctly. I never cared for him, but Susan—his wife, and my friend—seemed happy enough. Anna being an only child, the house went to Edward, the next brother. They might have lived with him but Pamela, the youngest sibling, invited Susan to bring Anna to live with her. She was married to a naval captain, and she welcomed the companionship while her husband was away at sea. James and Emily are their children."

Philip frowned, trying to keep track of the names.

"Don't worry about remembering all the details," Aunt Beth added, as if she'd read his mind. "I'm just giving you the overall picture.

Philip nodded; he was following so far. "If Anna went to her aunt, why was she living with Edward Tremayne four years ago?"

"The children's father was killed in the East Indies a couple of years after Anna's father died, then her aunt and mother both succumbed to the influenza. About eight years ago now."

Four years before they'd met.

"Anna did go to Edward then, with the children. The poor mites needed someone they knew, losing both parents so close together. She's been the nearest thing to a mother they've had ever since."

"Good heavens." She'd lost her father, then her mother and aunt. Eight years ago? She must have been young then, only around seventeen. "You said her father was one of four children."

"Yes. The third brother is dead, too, but he left a son and a couple of daughters. Josiah, the son, is married. He and Diana have three or four brats—and I use that term advisedly."

"So she was living with Edward when she married?"

Aunt Beth stood. "No. He died not long after you went to the Caribbean. But you should ask her to tell you the rest of the story. She married in a hurry. I also know that the lack of communication from you distressed her greatly."

He would normally consider a married woman pining for a letter from another man as unfaithful, in wish if not in deed. Perhaps the poison of that letter was leaving him, for his first thought was not that, but to wonder about the circumstances of her marriage.

He closed his eyes against the thought that she had been forced into it. "Did you meet her husband?" He asked the question, although he wasn't sure he wanted to hear the answer.

"Yes, I did. He was a good man, Philip…"

That's what Anna had said, at the inn.

"…but again, you must ask her if you want to know more. I will consider who might have written that letter to you, but now I really must get back to Cook."

Philip continued to sit there after his aunt left, gazing into the fire. Anna must be a stronger woman than he'd ever suspected, with all those changes in her young life. And although Aunt Beth hadn't said so directly, she clearly believed that there had been a good reason for her marriage.

He bent his head down until it rested in his hands. His

lack of trust had probably destroyed whatever might have been between them.

Could it be mended? He hoped so, but he should, at the very least, apologise.

He would find her and do that.

CHAPTER 5

*P*hilip found Lizzie adorning mantelpieces and pictures in the parlour with the evergreens they'd gathered that morning. Anna was not with them, nor was she helping Catherine and Thalia weave kissing balls in the dining room. Becoming concerned, for it was cold outside, Philip questioned the butler and footman. Neither of them had seen Anna return, and the maid sent to look in her room reported that she was not there.

He had a little more luck in the stables—one of the grooms thought he'd seen a female figure walking along the hill, heading east. He remembered a route they'd taken together several times, and hurried back to his room to collect his greatcoat and hat. Dusk would fall early with the thickening clouds, and the faint yellow tinge to the light spoke of snow to come. It would not do for her to be out alone as darkness fell, and who knew how far she might have walked. And it was his fault that she had gone off as she had.

Rather than follow her, he set off to walk the route in reverse. Tiny flakes fell from the sky, drifting around in the still air and melting when they touched the ground.

The path divided not far into the trees. He hesitated, unsure which to take, and wondering whether he was making too much of her absence. She was a sensible woman, probably more so than he'd realised, and would return before dark. On the other hand, even sensible women could have mishaps. But as those considerations went through his mind he caught a glimpse of movement through the trees.

He knew the moment Anna spotted him. She hesitated, then put her chin up and carried on walking.

"Captain." She nodded, her expression polite and as cold as the winter air. She stepped sideways to walk around him.

His heart sank. "Anna, please wait a moment."

She stopped, but did not turn to face him.

"Anna, I'm sorry for what I said earlier—it was totally unjustified."

"Thank you." Her tone was flat, as if his apology didn't really matter.

"Are you returning to the house? May I walk with you?"

She hesitated. "If you wish."

It was not an enthusiastic acceptance, but she *had* agreed. He moved beside her and held his arm out, but she ignored him and walked on. That hurt, but after what he'd said he couldn't blame her.

"Anna, may we talk?"

"We are talking now, are we not?" She didn't pause, or look at him. "If you only came to apologise for your slur on my character, you have done so."

"I didn't. I mean, that was not the only reason. I wanted to explain my actions."

They were out of the trees now, fatter white flakes swirling around them in a rising breeze. She stopped and faced him, her lips set in a hard line. "You denied me an opportunity to explain, yet expect me to listen to you?"

"Not expect, no. Hope. Hope that you will give me another chance."

Anna finally looked away as his gaze did not waver. If she refused, she would be as much to blame for the end of their friendship as he. For the end of any possibility of more.

"Very well, I will listen. But not here—after dinner, perhaps. Or tomorrow."

"Thank you." He held his arm out again, and this time she took it.

"I wrote to you from Antigua, as soon as the *Garnet* arrived. Did you receive that?"

"No." She remembered how she'd calculated the length of the *Garnet*'s Atlantic voyage, the time it would take for mail to return, schooling herself not to look for a letter until there was a reasonable possibility of its arriving. Then Uncle Edward had died and she'd had to put it to the back of her mind. "At least, not unless Diana took it. It's just the kind of thing she might do."

"Diana?"

"That's part of my explanation, Captain. Now is not the time for that, either."

But he was not to be put off, it seemed. "Anna, when we met at the inn, you said you'd sent me two letters. Am I recalling correctly?"

Why did that matter?

"Yes. I sent the first via the Admiralty, as you said. When there was no reply I wrote again, but sent it to Aunt Beth to forward, in case your situation had changed." She preferred not to remember those anxious months of waiting.

"Ah."

"What do you mean?"

His lips curved a little, a hint of the teasing smile she

remembered—the one that said he knew she would be amused too. "The 'ah' is part of *my* explanation, which you do not want to hear yet."

"Philip! You are just as annoying as ever!" She still wanted to be angry with him, but instead was irritated at the feelings his smile could still arouse.

"It is a very short explanation, Anna. Will you not hear it now?"

A sudden gust blew snow into their faces. "Inside," she said.

"Come on, then." He took her hand and hurried her along until they arrived, breathless, at the back of the house. Smells of roasting meat and gingerbread filled the air as he looked into rooms along the servants' corridor, finally pulling her into the stillroom and closing the door. "We may be private here for a few minutes."

She stripped off her gloves and pulled her bonnet ribbons undone, seeing from the sudden intensity in his expression that he, too, was remembering that day when they'd kissed.

Would he do it again, now? She shouldn't want him to.

He took a step back.

"Anna." He appeared to be bracing himself. "Before your letter arrived, I received one from Aunt Beth. One I *thought* was from Aunt Beth. It described your marriage in the most unflattering terms possible. I know now that Beth did not write it." He glanced away, before meeting her gaze again. "Anna, I should not have accepted that correspondence at face value, and I am ashamed of myself for doing so. It was not long after that when your first letter arrived."

What would she have thought, if she'd received such a letter about him? Doubted her judgement of his character, probably.

"It doesn't excuse me," he said, "but I hope it explains a little."

"It does, yes." It also went a long way to excusing him, but she wasn't quite ready to admit that yet.

Philip let out a breath. "Thank you."

"What was the 'ah' for, Philip?"

"My note of your address got wet and the ink ran, so rather than risk misdirecting it I sent my letter from Antigua here for Beth to forward. Your second letter to me also came here."

She frowned. "Someone here kept them?"

"It seems likely."

She nodded. "I sent a short note to Aunt Beth before my marriage. I wonder if someone read that before Aunt Beth received it, and wrote to you pretending to be her."

"Probably. I find it hard to believe that any of my cousins could do such a thing, but someone did. Aunt Beth is thinking about who the culprit might be."

"Good." It was too late to change the past, but it might help if they knew why someone had tried to make trouble between them.

Philip stepped forwards, reaching out and touching her arm. "Anna, you said we did not know each other well. That is true, but may we try to get to know each other better? We have twelve days here."

"I can't stay until Twelfth Night, Philip. I have to go back to Weymouth."

"Why? Oh, your cousins?"

"Yes."

"Aunt Beth told me something of your background. Will you tell me the rest? We have a few days, at least."

"If you still wish to know." She did owe him an explanation for her actions.

"I do. Thank you."

She held her hand out, but instead of shaking it he raised it to his lips. Her cheeks heated as she pulled her hand away, fumbling to unlatch the door before hurrying upstairs to her room. Being in the same house with Philip was no longer something to be avoided, but she already felt guilty about not spending Christmas Day with James and Emily. She could not stay longer.

Even if she could, she wasn't sure that she should.

It seemed Aunt Beth's supervisory activities were over, for Philip found her in the parlour with her feet up on a stool and a cup of tea in one hand. The mistletoe ball that Catherine and Thalia had been making hung from the small chandelier in the centre of the room, and swags of holly and ivy decorated the mantelpiece and picture frames.

"The girls have done well, don't you think, Philip?" She cocked her head to one side at the sound of over-loud male voices in the hall. "Ah, the Yule log finally arrives. Well, we'll have a few minutes peace while they get it into the drawing room fireplace. Do sit down."

He took a chair facing her, unsure how to begin.

"Have you made your peace with Anna yet?"

He should have known she'd ask that. "I've started," he said. "But I came to ask you about a letter."

"Another letter?" Her brows rose and she took a sip of tea.

"Yes. Anna said she sent a second letter to me via you, but I only received one."

"That would be Thalia, I expect." Her brow creased, a mix of annoyance and sorrow.

Philip gaped for a moment at her instant conclusion. "Are you sure? Have you spoken to her?"

Beth shook her head. "No, and I do not intend to raise the subject until Anna has left."

"How do you know Thalia kept it back?"

"I only suspect at the moment, after what you told me earlier. But I have been thinking about it, and I don't see who else it could have been. I doubt that Anna confided in anyone at home about her feelings for you, let alone details of your posting. It has to be someone in this house, and most likely the same person who wrote that unpleasant letter to you. I don't want to believe there are two members of my family acting in such an underhand way."

She set her cup down and swung her feet to the floor, sitting up straight. "Philip, did you flirt with Thalia that summer? Or say anything that might make her think you particularly liked her?"

"Good grief, no. She was just a child."

"Fifteen is old enough for her to have started thinking about potential suitors."

Philip tried to recall. "She did come with us sometimes, when we took Anna's cousins up on the downs. I just assumed the other children here at the time were too young for her."

Beth sat back. "A natural assumption. I'm guessing she was jealous of the attention you paid to Anna."

That could also explain her sulks and flirting today. And that comment about prize money that he'd been stupid enough to repeat to Anna.

"Philip, I cannot say how sorry I am for the distress those letters have caused the pair of you. If it was Thalia, it's possible she may try to stir up more trouble, but I will keep a close eye on her. If I confront her now, there'll be tantrums that could spoil everyone's Christmas and make things very uncomfortable for Anna, and for you."

She had a point. "Aunt Beth, may I tell Anna what you suspect?"

"By all means. Part of Thalia's punishment, if she is the

one, should be to see that her stratagem has failed. Now go and change for dinner while I finish my tea."

Philip gave her his best salute, and she laughed as she shooed him away.

∽

Sitting before the mirror as Aunt Beth's maid arranged her hair, Anna found that she was looking forward to dinner. At least Philip had agreed to hear her explanation—had even asked her to explain. Whether he would accept her reasons for breaking her promise to him remained to be seen, but she would face that tomorrow.

Aunt Beth's children had been almost as close as brother and sisters to her on the visits she'd made during her childhood. Now she could enjoy a family Christmas Eve dinner with them all.

She smoothed her gown as she walked downstairs, knowing its gold silk with a paler net overdress became her well. The maid had woven matching ribbons into her hair, and added a small sprig of holly to acknowledge the season.

A hubbub of chatter already filled the drawing room when she entered, and the air held the spicy scent of mulled wine. Uncle Thomas handed her a glass and she sipped it, feeling the warmth spreading through her. She admired the huge log blazing in the fireplace, still amused by everyone's pretence that it had taken the menfolk all day to find it. Only a few minutes later, Bates announced that dinner was served.

"Let me escort you in, my dear Anna," Uncle Thomas said, holding his arm so she could lay her hand upon it. "Beth has decreed that you shall keep me company and tell me all about young James and how he is enjoying school."

Uncle Thomas took the seat at the head of the table, with Anna beside him. Aunt Beth and Philip had the equivalent positions at the far end of the dining table. Anna wasn't sorry —although she had made her peace with him, it was too soon in their mending relationship to be thrown together.

"Bless me, Cook has done us proud again," Uncle Thomas said, regarding the array of dishes spread before them. "Although I'll warrant this is nothing to our Christmas feast tomorrow. Now, what can I help you to, my dear? A slice of pheasant? Some of these excellent beans?"

Anna allowed Uncle Thomas to serve her. "Not too much, Uncle. I'm sure there are some tasty desserts to come." As they ate the first course their talk turned to how James and Emily were getting on, and the doings of the various Kempton grandchildren then took them through the rest of the meal.

Bursts of laughter came from the other end of the table, where a cheerful-looking Philip seemed to be keeping his neighbours entertained. Thalia, in particular, was regarding him with a coy expression, although Anna could not see that he was returning the attention. Then his gaze met her own and the warm smile that spread across his face could have been one from four years ago.

The Kemptons never stood on ceremony, regularly talking across the table, so Anna wasn't surprised when Uncle Thomas raised his voice a little and asked Philip what he intended to do with himself now the war was over.

"For there'll be less call for naval men, I should think. Will they give you another frigate?"

"They might, Uncle, but there are captains senior to me, and more experienced, wanting ships as well."

"We've been following your exploits in the papers, Phil," Toby said. "You must have made a fair bit of prize money. Enough to live on?"

Anna listened with interest. For her own sanity, she had stopped reading naval reports from the Caribbean, trusting that Aunt Beth would tell her if Philip had been badly injured or killed.

"I could buy a small estate with it," Philip said. "And put some in the five percents. I'd get by tolerably well."

"You, a farmer?" Toby laughed. "I can't see you being happy in one place."

Anna thought he might do very well as a landowner. From what she remembered so vividly of their time together, he loved being in the countryside. But Toby had known Philip from their childhoods—he must understand him much better than she did.

"I'd miss the sea, certainly," Philip admitted. "I haven't decided yet—there is no pressing need to do so, after all."

It sounded as if he'd take another command if one were to be offered. Anna turned her gaze to the plate before her, her appetite for the trifle fading. She stabbed her spoon in, annoyed with herself for wishing that Philip would find a way to stay in the country. All she had hoped for from this visit was to clear up the misunderstanding between them.

"How about standing for parliament?" Uncle Thomas suggested. "They could do with some men of sense in the Commons."

Entering politics was an idea that Philip had toyed with, but it didn't appeal to him.

"I could help you if you decide to go that route, Philip," Anthony put in. "I know a few people with influence."

"Thanks, Tony, but—"

'Well, if you men are going to talk politics, I think it's time we retired to the drawing room." Aunt Beth stood as she spoke. "Don't be too long now, or I will have to come and fetch you." She wagged a finger at her husband. Uncle Thomas laughed.

Thank goodness for that—at last he would be free of Thalia's flirtatious comments and fluttering eyelashes. He studiously ignored her parting smile as she followed her mother out of the room, watching Anna instead. Their eyes had met a few times during the meal and, to his delight, his smiles had elicited answering ones, and even a blush. Now, though, she did not look at him as she left the room.

Damn. Something had upset her, but he had no idea what it could be.

"Philip?"

"What?" He looked up from his plate to find all eyes on him. "My apologies, I was distracted."

"Have some more wine," Anthony said, passing the decanter. Philip poured a little into his glass, but did not drink.

"So, might you stand for a seat in parliament, Philip?" Uncle Thomas persisted.

"It doesn't appeal to me, Uncle. Too much corruption involved at the ballot."

"Fair point," Anthony said.

"It has been suggested I could join the diplomatic service," Philip said, recalling the letter from Lord Harpenden that he still hadn't given much consideration to.

Toby snorted. "Diplomacy, Phil? Really?"

"Don't judge him by yourself, my boy," Uncle Thomas said, and Toby gave a wry smile.

"What prompted that idea?" Anthony asked, his face serious. "I've heard of admirals having to deal with political matters, but a captain? Not that I'm impugning your abilities in any way, you understand."

"I'm not sure," Philip replied. There had been several incidents when he'd become involved in dealings with the governors of Caribbean islands, but he didn't want to start lengthy explanations at the moment.

"Are you going to join the Boxing Day hunt?" Toby asked Anthony. "I've a new hunter…"

Philip stopped listening as the others embarked on a detailed discussion of the merits of their own mounts. He was hoping to get Anna to himself after dinner, and perhaps hear her explanation.

Finally losing patience, he pushed his chair back. "If you will excuse me, gentlemen, I will join the ladies."

"We all will," Uncle Thomas said, getting to his feet.

Good. He just hoped Anna had not yet retired to her room.

CHAPTER 6

*I*n the drawing room, Lizzie was arranging chairs around the circular table, a deck of cards ready in its centre. Philip's spirits sank as he realised that Anna was not here—but then neither was Aunt Beth.

Uncle Thomas paused beside him as the others entered the room. "Anna and Beth will be in the parlour," he said quietly.

"We thought we'd play Speculation," Lizzie said, "but I can get the Pope Joan board out if you prefer?"

"Speculation will do nicely." Anthony sat down at the table and rubbed his hands. "Prepare to lose money to me, wife!"

"Ha!" Lizzie replied with a grin.

"I'm for the parlour." Uncle Thomas patted his stomach. "Takes time to digest at my age, you know."

"I'll join you, if I may?" Philip said. Hopefully Anna would be there, but if not it might be useful to have a serious discussion with Uncle Thomas about his possible futures.

"I'll come as well, Papa." Thalia had approached them without Philip noticing. "Speculation is a childish game."

Uncle Thomas regarded her with raised brows. "You've always enjoyed it before, Thalia. Are you feeling quite well?"

Thalia's eyelashes fluttered as she glanced at Philip before facing her father. "Of course I am well, Papa."

Philip tried not to show his irritation. He'd retire to his room if necessary—he was not going to sit through yet more flirting.

"I'm sure you must be unwell, Thalia," Uncle Thomas said, his voice devoid of sympathy. "If you aren't feeling up to a game, perhaps you should retire to your room."

At another time, the chagrin in Thalia's face might have been amusing.

"I'll ask Bates to get some hot milk sent up," Uncle Thomas added. "It's what your mama has when she's indisposed."

Thalia's mouth fell open for a moment. "Oh, very well, I'll play, but I shan't enjoy it!"

"Come, Philip." Uncle Thomas clapped him on the shoulder and headed for the parlour without waiting to see what his daughter did. "She can sulk to her heart's content—the others will take no notice." He opened the parlour door, Philip letting out a breath of relief as he saw Anna sitting with Aunt Beth near the fire.

"You were right about what Thalia would do, my dear," Uncle Thomas said as he sat down near his wife.

Aunt Beth nodded, her lips pursing briefly before she smiled at Philip. "You are welcome to join us." She glanced at Anna. "Unless the two of you wish for private conversation."

"I would, if that suits Anna," Philip said, still concerned by Anna's lack of a smile.

Anna stood. "Very well, Captain. Shall we go to the library?"

Captain? She had called him Philip this afternoon.

. . .

The library was dim, its fire burning low. Anna lit more lamps while Philip added logs to the fire. She took a seat, declining Philip's offer of a glass of port. She'd had enough wine at dinner, and wanted to keep a clear head now—both to explain things properly, and to guard her own emotions. She did not want to rekindle all the feelings she'd had for him.

"Will you tell me about your husband, Anna?" Philip sat down. "You said he was a good man."

"And that he was three times my age. In fact, he was older still." Anna gazed at him, her eyes narrowed. The difference in their ages was one of the things he'd thrown at her in the woods this morning.

"Go on."

There was nothing in his expression beyond polite enquiry; the tension in her shoulders relaxed.

"You said he was a good man," he prompted again.

"He was. I met him just after my mother died and I went to live with my Uncle Edward, but I'd known of him for a couple of years before that. This was all a few years before you and I met."

"Aunt Beth gave me some of your family history," Philip said. "But she told me nothing about Lord Radnor."

Anna shook her head. "Not Lord Radnor. Admiral Sir Alastair Radnor."

"Admiral Radnor?"

"You've heard of him?"

"Indeed, yes. He's—he *was*—well-respected in naval circles."

"Well, Captain Severin, the children's father, had come to Alastair's notice when he was but a midshipman. Alastair acted as a kind of sponsor, I think. Later, when he married, Severin asked if Alastair would see that his family were looked after if anything should happen to him."

61

"A guardian?"

"Not formally, no. Unfortunately. Alastair wrote regularly after Captain Severin died," she went on, "although he never came to see us. I was living with Mama and Aunt Pamela then, in Plymouth."

"Then your mother and aunt died."

"Yes. I went back to live with my uncle in Yeovil, with the children. James was six then, and Emily only four. That was where I grew up, but Papa willed it to Uncle Edward, rather than to my mother."

"Your uncle treated you well?"

"Oh, yes. That is to say, he meant well, but he was a confirmed bachelor and spent most of his time shut up in his study. He had no idea what to do with small children."

"I understand you live in Weymouth now. Was that where Radnor lived?"

"Yes—Yeovil is but thirty miles from it, much closer than Plymouth. I wrote to inform him of our change of circumstances. I was hoping he might visit, but I heard nothing for nearly a month."

The letters Alastair had written to Pamela after Severin's death had been friendly, showing what Anna felt to be genuine concern for the wellbeing of the children and their mother. Still distraught at the deaths of her mother and aunt, Anna had longed for someone to confide in and consult.

"That must have been a difficult time for you."

Anna looked up to find Philip's gaze fixed on her face. His tone was gentle, full of sympathy.

"It was." She rubbed her temple—it didn't seem right to speak ill of the dead, but her family's failings were pertinent to her story. "Mama always said the Tremaynes were hopeless with money—Uncle Edward certainly was. I had a little from what Papa had left to Mama, but he had made no specific provision for me. Captain Severin was more sensible

—he set up a trust for his children. A solicitor in London arranged for funds to be paid to my uncle, but I discovered the housekeeper was diverting some of it into her own pocket."

"Your uncle did not object?"

"He only wanted a quiet life, and doubted what I was telling him. Besides which, the woman appeared to have Uncle Edward pretty well under her thumb. That money was intended for the children, so I wrote to Sir Alastair again."

That second letter had produced results.

Uncle Edward's manservant knocked on the door. Anna looked up from the account book she was trying to decipher.

"There's a Mr Donaldson to see you, Miss. Says he's come from Admiral Radnor."

Anna felt a mixture of relief that the admiral had finally responded to her letters, and dread in case something had happened to him.

"Please show him into the parlour." Anna closed the account book and checked that her hair was tidy before going to meet her visitor.

Donaldson stood and made a small bow as Anna entered the parlour. He was nearly as old as Uncle Edward, and much thinner, with black hair just beginning to grey at the temples and a weather-beaten face. "Miss Tremayne, Admiral Radnor has sent me in answer to your second letter."

"Is he well, Mr Donaldson? Do, please, sit down."

Donaldson shrugged as he resumed his seat. "He is never entirely well, Miss Tremayne, but he is much as usual. Shortly after your first communication, the admiral sent you an invitation to visit him in Weymouth. From your recent letter, it appears you never received it."

"No, I did not."

"Sir Alastair asked me to repeat the invitation in person. Unfortunately he is not fit to travel himself."

"I'm sorry to hear it." That would explain why he had never suggested visiting them at Plymouth.

"Would it be possible for you and the children to accompany me to Weymouth for the day tomorrow? We will return you here tomorrow evening."

That would be a long day, but it would be better than having to stay somewhere overnight.

"I will be happy to accept the admiral's invitation, as long as my uncle has no objection."

"Thank you, Miss Tremayne. If Mr Tremayne cannot spare you, a note to the Mermaid will reach me." He stood as he spoke, and made another small bow before leaving.

Uncle Edward's study door stood open; Anna could see him sitting near the window, his spectacles balanced on the end of his nose. He looked up at her knock, and placed a finger in his book to keep his place.

"Anna, what is it? Who was that caller?"

Taking this as permission to enter, Anna made her way past the desk piled with dusty books and letters, and the stack of newspapers on the floor.

"It was a Mr Donaldson, Uncle, come from Admiral Radnor. He stands sponsor to James and Emily, you recall."

"Radnor? Oh, yes." He gazed at her over his spectacles, one brow raised in enquiry.

"The admiral invites me and the children to visit him tomorrow." She briefly explained the arrangements before her uncle could protest that there was no carriage to take her.

"Very well, I see no objection." Uncle Edward nodded, and turned back to his book.

"Uncle." Anna waited until he looked up again—it hadn't

taken her long to realise that he heard nothing unless she had his full attention.

"What is it? I've said you—"

"Uncle, Mr Donaldson said the admiral wrote to me a month ago, but I did not receive a letter."

"A letter? A month… Ah!" This time Uncle Edward put a marker in his book and closed it with a sigh. He heaved himself out of the chair and crossed to the desk. After much moving of books and papers, and several sneezes, he finally held out a sealed letter to Anna. "There, I knew it would be here somewhere. I must have forgotten to give it to you."

He looked so pleased to have found it that Anna didn't have the heart to ask him to be more careful in future. She thanked him, and went to ensure that in future the manservant would deliver all the post to her.

James and Emily were still missing their mother, and even new sights along the road to Weymouth the next morning did little to divert them. James, at least, cheered up when they came in sight of the sea and they could smell the salt in the air.

The coach halted on a road between the sands and a terraced row of houses. Anna noted three floors, and windows for servants' quarters in the roof. The brass knocker on the front door shone, and the two windows beside it were spotless.

"Welcome, Miss Tremayne." A stately butler bowed in the open doorway, and stood to one side to usher her in. "Master James, Miss Emily."

James chuckled as the butler bowed to him as well but Emily just clutched Anna's hand more tightly. The furnishings in the hall were sparse and functional, but as spic and span as the outside.

"My name is Bradley, Miss Tremayne. Sir Alastair asked

me to show you to his parlour. He would like to see you first, while Donaldson takes the children upstairs."

"Sir Alastair has a telescope set up to look at ships," Donaldson said, and James's doubtful expression cleared.

"Look after your sister, James," Anna added as she followed Bradley into a bright and airy parlour.

Sir Alastair sat in a wheeled chair near the window, a blanket draped over his legs. He had a full head of white hair, tied neatly back. Anna thought at first that he wore a wig, as would have been the fashion when he was younger, but there were no rolls above his ears. His face was gaunt and lined, nearly as pale as his hair and with shadows beneath his eyes.

She crossed the room and made her curtsey.

"Welcome, my dear. I am glad to meet you at last." His voice was stronger than Anna expected, but the hand he waved trembled slightly. "Your aunt thought highly of you, from what she wrote in her letters. And now you have charge of her children."

"Yes, sir. In a manner of speaking." Anna took the seat indicated.

Sir Alastair gestured towards the blanket. "You will see why I have not been able to visit. Now, tell me how things are, and why I received no reply to my invitation a month ago."

Anna haltingly described Uncle Edward's household, and her worries about the children's trust fund. Sir Alastair nodded and asked pertinent questions; his physical frailty did not appear to have affected his mind.

"Do you think your uncle intends to make his own use of the children's trust fund?" he asked.

Anna had considered that question over the last few weeks. She shook her head. "No. He is well intentioned, but too..." Lazy or selfish sounded very harsh. "To be plain, sir, I think my uncle is far too disorganised to manage any fraudulent scheme, even if he wished to."

"Ha, yes, he sounds that way. Let me think about it, my dear. In the meantime, please ask Bradley to have the children brought down."

A maid with a tea tray followed the children into the room, and Anna poured while James enthused about the telescope Donaldson had shown him, and the ships 'just like Papa's' that he'd seen moored in the bay. Emily was more interested in a portrait of the admiral over the fireplace, asking if Papa's uniform had looked like that. She moved on to examine a model ship in a glass case and demanded to know why there weren't any people on it. Sir Alastair conversed easily with them, and they seemed to like him.

Philip listened as much to Anna's tone as to the words she spoke. Her great affection for the admiral was clear, but her description of his age and frail health removed most of the jealousy he felt.

"We stayed the whole day," she continued. "We went to see him often after that, usually once a month. He even came out with us a few times, for a carriage ride to the Isle of Portland or to Chesil Bank." She chuckled. "James was not impressed by the beach there—he complained that he couldn't make castles out of pebbles."

That reminded Philip of the ten-year-old James he'd helped with the chalk dog. The lad would be fourteen now. "Did Sir Alastair help you sort out the problem with the housekeeper?"

Anna smiled, a wry curve of her lips. "In a way. Donaldson was his man of business; he came several times to go through Uncle Edward's accounts with me. We didn't accuse her of theft, but I showed Uncle the books and explained how the housekeeper could save a great deal of money by changing suppliers."

"She was making her own profits?"

"Clearly, yes. It's quite common where there is no one to supervise. This time Uncle Edward listened to me, and when he told her to change she resigned in a fit of pique. The only problem with that was that my uncle decided I knew enough to become the housekeeper myself."

Edward Tremayne was long dead, but Philip still felt anger growing at the man for taking advantage of his niece. Something must have shown on his face.

"Oh, I didn't mind, Philip. It kept me busy, and I learned a lot. I had very little money of my own, and running his household meant I could save it for the future instead of contributing for my keep."

From what Aunt Beth had told him, Edward had died shortly after Philip had received his urgent summons back to Portsmouth. That must have been the event that led to her marriage, although surely Aunt Beth would have offered her a home if her uncle had not left her enough to support herself.

Anna was gazing into the fire, a soft smile on her face as if she was remembering pleasant times. She looked up, and her smile took his breath away. He just hoped some of it was for him, and not all for her late husband.

"Uncle Edward…" Her voice broke off as they heard voices in the hallway, then Toby burst in.

"What are you two doing here? We need you to make up the numbers for cards."

Philip glanced at Anna, wanting to hear the rest of her explanation. But tomorrow would be soon enough—he knew now that there must have been a good reason for the marriage.

"Do you feel like joining the others?" he asked.

She smiled, and took his arm as she stood.

CHAPTER 7

*P*hilip did not manage to get Anna alone until the next afternoon. Snow had fallen overnight, and everyone had been ferried to the village church in their carriages for the Christmas Day service. Then he had to sit through the feast that Aunt Beth had arranged. At any other time he would have enjoyed the roast goose and venison, vegetables, jellies, creams, and plum pudding; now, he just wanted the chance to talk to Anna alone again.

The meal finally over, Aunt Beth and Uncle Thomas retired to the parlour to doze the afternoon away, and his cousins headed for the billiards room or the nursery to play with their children. Philip followed Anna to the library.

She sat near the window, watching as snow started to drift down again, pale against the grey clouds. A small crease between her brows gave her a pensive, almost worried, look.

He drew up a chair to sit close to her. "Is something troubling you?"

She looked at him, smoothing her expression. "I promised to return home the day after tomorrow, so I could spend some of the festive season with the children. It looks as if that may not be possible."

So soon? She'd said she couldn't stay until Twelfth Night, but he'd hoped to have a few more days. "It's no deeper than it was this morning," he said. "And it isn't freezing—the snow may not lie for long."

"I hope you're right." She did look a little more cheerful. Her gaze turned to the window again, although approaching dusk meant that little was visible through the reflections in the glass. "I wish I'd brought them along. They would have enjoyed the gardens and downs, even in this weather. Emily would love Aunt Beth's decorations. But under the circumstances..."

Guilt over his past behaviour stabbed him again. She'd come expecting that she might be upset and hadn't wanted to show it in front of her cousins.

"We have a little time before we're expected to eat again," he said. He glanced around, although he would have heard if anyone else had come into the room. "Will you tell me the rest of your story?"

Anna looked at her hands for a moment, then drew a deep breath. "Uncle Edward died at the end of October, only a few months after we met."

He nodded. "Aunt Beth told me that. I suppose the house went to your remaining uncle?" He frowned, trying to recall exactly what Beth had said. "No, his son?"

"Yes. Cousin Josiah. For, naturally, Uncle Edward considered that women are not mentally equipped to hold property themselves."

He couldn't make out if her tone was one of bitterness or sarcasm—whichever it was, he sympathised. "In spite of the fact that you'd been managing his household accounts far better than he ever had."

Something in her relaxed, and she smiled. "Indeed.

Cousin Josiah chose to live there and sell his previous dwelling, and was quite happy for me to continue my duties as housekeeper."

"Without pay, naturally."

The corners of her mouth turned down as she nodded. "That wouldn't have been so bad, except for Diana—his wife. Everything had to be done her way, even things that had been running perfectly well before, and nothing was ever good enough for her or her children."

"Aunt Beth referred to them as brats," he put in, remembering Beth's expression as she said it.

"I would describe them as spoiled bullies," Anna said bluntly. "Within a day, Emily had her hair pulled and her favourite doll taken. James had been punished for trying to defend her."

An unenviable situation to have been left in. "Aunt Beth would have been happy to have you live here," he suggested.

"She would, yes. She said as much, after... after my marriage. But I couldn't leave the children. I couldn't protect them if I stayed, either, not when Diana believed everything her offspring told her, even the most obvious lies."

That made sense—but she could have brought them here with her. Aunt Beth loved having family around her, the more the better. "Why didn't you ask...?" His voice tailed off as something nudged at his memory. "The trust fund?"

"Yes. They—Josiah and Diana—decided that their sons should share James' tutor, at no cost to themselves, and that James didn't really need to start attending the school Donaldson had helped to arrange for him."

Her lips compressed as she spoke, and Philip guessed there were other ways in which her relatives had made life unpleasant for her and her charges. He clenched a fist, wishing he could plant it in the face of this Cousin Josiah.

"If the children were not living with them, there would be

no reason for the solicitor to pay money from their trust fund to Josiah. Although I'd been acting as their guardian, it was not a formal arrangement. If I'd tried to move them here —or anywhere else—Josiah would have had little difficulty in convincing others that he should remain in charge of them."

"Uncle Thomas…" He knew as he said it that it was not a possible solution. "Josiah is a relative, and Thomas is not."

"Exactly"

"But Admiral Radnor was not a relative, either."

"Ah, but he had money, a title, and influence. So, you see, I did marry for a title and money, just as that letter said."

Anna waited while Philip considered her words, her stomach fluttering.

"The motive makes all the difference," he said, although he spoke slowly. As if he were thinking of something else.

"It was not an easy decision to make, Philip," she added, but he appeared abstracted still.

She did not want to sit and wait for his verdict. "I will see you later," she said, rising from her chair and smoothing her skirts. She hoped they had made enough progress that he would still speak to her, even if he did not accept her reasons for breaking her promise.

"Anna."

She turned to face him.

"Thank you for telling me." There was little indication in his face about what he thought, what he felt.

Anna retreated to her bedroom and sat on the window seat, watching the snow again. In spite of what Philip had said, she did think it was settling. The lines of the clipped hedges in the formal gardens below had blurred as snow collected on their tops.

The friends that James and Emily were staying with lived

not far from Weymouth, and Anna had arranged to send word when she had returned. No harm would come to them if she was a day or two late, but they were expecting her and she did not want to disappoint them.

There was no reason for her to stay here beyond Boxing Day. Philip would either accept her explanation or not, and she would discover which next time they encountered each other—this evening, probably. She wished his approbation didn't matter so much to her, but it did. The heaviness in her stomach was nothing to do with the Christmas feast she'd merely picked at.

Her decision to marry hadn't been taken lightly. Sir Alastair, seated in his usual chair overlooking the bay, had explained how he could apply to the Court of Chancery to become the children's guardian—he could easily afford the necessary expenses.

"But I have no legal remit from Severin," he finished. "Your cousin could contest the case on the grounds that he is kin. But if we were married, that argument would be largely negated. It would be a marriage in name only, my dear."

She stared out to sea, trying to think through the practical implications of his suggestion. It was a way out of her predicament, and she believed his assurance that it would work, but her mind kept returning to the promise she'd given to Philip in the woodland glade.

Sir Alastair finally broke the long silence. "Anna, you know how sorry I am that you have been put in this situation. It was a dereliction of duty on your uncle's part not to have provided for you adequately, particularly as what he had came from your father."

"You are too kind, sir." As her memories of Papa had faded with time, she had come to resent his lack of forethought. "The original fault was my father's. He made no provision for a dowry for me, only the small income he left Mama that came to me on her death."

"A marriage between us would benefit me as well, you know," he said gently. "Who, in my situation, would not wish to have a beautiful young woman at his beck and call?"

The twinkle in his eye made her smile. She thought he would enjoy having all three of them in the house, as long as she ensured the children did not tire him. But she was still reluctant to break her promise, to obliterate the hope of a happy future with Philip.

Something of that must have shown in her face.

"Is there a young man involved?"

She felt her cheeks heat, and nodded. "Yes, but there is no formal arrangement."

"Can he not help you?"

"He is the second lieutenant in the *Garnet*, bound for the Caribbean. He expects to be away for at least a couple of years."

"Ah." He gazed out of the window, to where the sun sparkled on the sea. "It is not easy, being a naval wife."

Her face grew even hotter. "We had not discussed that, sir. We did not get that far." She almost told him that she had promised to wait, but the decision whether to keep her word should be hers alone.

"I was thinking of my own late wife."

The kindly, middle-aged lady in a miniature portrait the admiral kept on the mantelpiece.

"I did not see as much of her as I wished, nor did I know my children well, to my great regret. I did my duty to my country, and got great satisfaction from doing so, but that can come at a high price for one's family."

He appeared lost in reminiscence for a moment. Anna didn't speak.

"But that is just my experience, my dear, and not relevant to your decision. Do bear in mind that even the most optimistic of my physicians give me no more than a couple of years. You are likely to be a widow by the time your young man returns."

She swallowed against a sudden lump in her throat. She knew he was ill, that was obvious, but he seemed not to mind that he was dying.

"No, do not look so upset, Anna. I've had a long life, and a useful one. Apart from not knowing my family better, my only regret in leaving this Earth would be that I hadn't done better to keep my word to Severin. He was a promising officer when I met him, and a good man."

Anna sat up straighter in her chair. "Sir, that is tantamount to…" She bit her lips against further words.

"Blackmail?" He had that twinkle in his eye again. "Manipulation? Perhaps it is. But tell me, if you explained all the circumstances to your young man, do you think he would understand?"

Would he? She hoped so, but she didn't know. Philip could not help her himself—even if he were here and willing to take on both her and the children, he might not be able to obtain guardianship. He was away doing his duty for the country. Looking after James and Emily was her duty. It was not as if Sir Alastair had proposed a full marriage, after all. There would be no consummation.

"Very well. Thank you, Sir Alastair."

There had been repercussions at home, of course. Josiah and Diana had ranted about her lack of family feeling, and were even less inclined to control their children's behaviour towards James and Emily. But all that was more bearable now they knew it would end soon, and it had taken

Donaldson little more than a week to arrange for a special licence and for their removal to Weymouth.

Looking out at the snow still falling, she thought that she could not regret her marriage to Alastair, even if Philip did not accept her explanation. Alastair had provided the help she needed to keep James and Emily safe and happy, but he'd been a good friend, too, in many ways. If she had not been blissfully happy with him, she had been content.

But she wanted more than just contentment.

She got to her feet abruptly. It was nearly time for supper, and to perhaps discover what Philip now thought about her.

Philip considered what Anna had said. She'd had no legal duty towards her young cousins, but the duty was there, nevertheless.

If he'd been in England at the time, he would have helped if he could, but there was no changing the past. The thought that she hadn't even asked him stung for a moment, until he put his emotions aside and considered the situation rationally. It would have taken many months for a letter to arrive and for him to reach England again. He couldn't even be sure that he would have returned—his own duty at the time had been to the Navy, and her need might not have persuaded his commanding officer to allow him leave.

Still trying to ignore his emotions, he wondered if it had been fair of him to ask for that promise. He'd been expecting to be away for a couple of years, but he knew full well that plans could change and some Navy men were away for much longer than that.

It was a lot to ask of a young woman, to wait for years without the security of a formal engagement. Even had he proposed marriage after only two weeks' acquaintance, it would still have been a lot to ask for. And she would then have been faced with the dilemma of breaking a formal engagement or allowing her cousins to be exploited and bullied.

There was nothing else she could have done. And if she could forgive his crediting that spiteful letter, he could surely forgive her justifiable breaking of her word.

Perhaps they could start again.

Aunt Beth had arranged a cold collation for their evening meal, to allow the servants to have their own feast below stairs. Anna had little appetite; she contemplated excusing herself, but she had to face Philip again at some time.

"Come, sit by me, Anna," Lizzie said as they entered the dining room. Philip had not yet arrived, so Anna took the seat between Lizzie and Toby. She was toying with a slice of ham when Philip spoke close behind her, making her jump.

"I don't see that you could have made any other decision," was all he said, his voice low enough that only she could hear it. There was no chance for more, as Anthony called him over with a question about horses and he took a seat further down the table.

He caught her eye, and his smile brought heat to her face. Taken with that, those few words were enough. The leaden feeling in her stomach dissipated, and she accepted an offer of chicken pie from Toby.

"So who's for the hunt tomorrow?" Anthony asked. "Anna, you don't care for it, I think?"

"No, thank you." She shook her head in emphasis. She could ride, but had no wish to jump hedges and gates.

"Philip? That was a fine hunter you arrived on."

"I'm not used to long hours in the saddle," Philip replied. "I'll have to decline this time." His eyes met Anna's again.

"Although I'll enjoy a ride out on the downs if anyone is interested."

She gave the smallest of nods—with any luck it would just be the two of them, and they would have more chance to talk. Then Lizzie spoke to her, and the rest of the meal passed quickly as Lizzie gave her all the news about her children.

"Think of something to do that doesn't involve moving," Toby groaned, sprawling in his chair an hour later. Looking around the parlour, Anna could see that everyone else felt much the same.

"You could read to us," Lizzie suggested. Anna suppressed a grimace—that would preclude any private conversation with Philip.

"Good idea," Toby said. "But not me, sister dear. I'd make a mull of it—that was very good Burgundy that Papa provided."

"We could read scenes from Shakespeare," Thalia suggested, "like we did last time Philip was here."

"I've no need to show off, Thally, but I don't mind if you do." Toby leaned his head on the back of the chair and closed his eyes.

Thalia sniffed, and turned her shoulder to her brother. "We could do Romeo and Juliet again, perhaps."

"I've always liked Much Ado About Nothing," Aunt Beth put in. "If read well, the banter between Beatrice and Benedick is most amusing."

"Oh, if we must do that play, I prefer the scenes between Claudio and Hero," Thalia said. She looked at Philip as she spoke, a coy smile on her face. Anna's eyes narrowed—the new understanding between her and Philip had put the deceitful letter-writer out of her head, but now she thought about it, Thalia was the obvious culprit. She'd cast other flirtatious looks at Philip these few days past.

"I'll read Hero, shall I?" Thalia's eyelashes fluttered again in Philip's direction.

"What, 'Leonato's short daughter'?" Toby sniggered.

Thalia's expression slipped for a moment. "A wronged maiden," she said. "There is no need to be rude, Toby. Philip, you should read Claudio."

Yes, it must have been Thalia. Anna sighed. She'd never been as close to Thalia as she was to Lizzie, because of the difference in their ages, but she hadn't expected such spite. What would Philip do at this blatant attempt at pairing the two of them off?

"If you wish," he said, sitting straighter in his chair. A happy smile spread across Thalia's face. Philip looked at her, his expression stern. "That seems most appropriate," he said. "I am, after all, a fool who believed a malicious fabrication against the woman I love."

Anna's breath caught as heat rose to her face. There had been an unmistakable note of sincerity in his voice. The silence in the room was almost palpable, all eyes on Philip.

Thalia lifted her chin. "Whatever do you mean, cousin?" But she didn't look puzzled, and her gaze slid away from Philip's face.

"I think you're more suited to Don John, Thalia. The architect of the lie."

Thalia's lips set in a hard line. "I didn't write anything that wasn't true."

"You lied about—"

"Philip, please." Anna's voice was quiet, but Philip stopped talking.

"Thalia, go to your bedroom," Aunt Beth ordered.

"But I didn't—"

"Now, Thalia!" Anna had never heard such command in Aunt Beth's voice. It appeared that Thalia hadn't either, for her mouth fell open.

Uncle Thomas stood. "Come with me, Thalia."

Thalia scowled at him, unmoving. He put one hand on her shoulder, waiting patiently until she turned and stalked out of the room. Anna didn't envy her the reckoning to come from Aunt Beth, but Thalia had brought it on herself, after all.

The air was thick with unasked questions. Anna decided it was best to give a straightforward explanation.

"Someone tried to make trouble between Philip and me four years ago," she said, her voice remarkably calm. "Through a letter that purported to come from Aunt Beth." From the silence, the others were reaching the same conclusion that she had come to.

"Cards, anyone?" Aunt Beth said. There was an instant murmur of agreement. "There are enough of us for two whist tables, when Thomas returns. Toby, rouse yourself and bring the small table over here."

Philip moved over to Anna's seat. She looked up at him with a smile and a shrug. "It seems we have been commanded," she said.

"Anna, I did not mean to distress you."

Warmth spread through her at the concern on his face. "You did not." Quite the opposite, in fact. "We are among friends, Philip," she added. "We have spent enough time alone together these few days that no one should be surprised there is something between us."

"Philip, Anna, come and join this table." Aunt Beth summoned them to one of the card tables.

"Can we talk tomorrow?" Philip asked as she stood up.

"Of course." She would look forward to it.

CHAPTER 8

*A*nna reined in Aunt Beth's docile mare as they reached the crest of the downs. Philip came to a halt beside her, close enough that their knees were almost touching. Below, the white landscape was intersected by the lines of hedges, black squares marking bare woodland. Thin lines of smoke rose from houses into the blue skies, and the horses' breath made frosty clouds in the still air. The faint sound of a hunting horn reached them, along with the baying of hounds.

"It will be melting by tomorrow," Philip said, his gaze to the south where a thin sheet of cloud was beginning to whiten the sky.

"How do you know?"

"You don't spend years at sea without learning something about the weather. Clouds like that often bring warmer air." He glanced at her, a wry smile on his face. "It will probably also bring rain, but if you must go tomorrow you should get home without too much difficulty."

"That's good." Except it didn't seem so, not now.

The whist last night had been a disaster; it was just as well they'd been playing for penny points. She'd done her best to concentrate on the game, to forget that he'd just announced that he loved her in front of everyone, but with little success. His smiles, the look in his eyes, were like those from four years ago. He laid down cards, and she'd looked at his hands, remembering how they had felt on hers. When he took a sip from his glass, her attention was on his lips, not which suit she should be playing. From the odd mutter of disgust from Toby or Lizzie, Philip's own play had been little better.

The party did not break up until late, and there'd been time only for him to quickly ask if she would walk or ride with him today before Aunt Beth shooed them all upstairs. She'd said goodnight to him in the parlour—after what she had been thinking, talking alone in a darkened corridor would not have been wise.

They had said little this morning as they mounted up; it hadn't seemed necessary. Just a few words as he'd adjusted the stirrup leather for her, then they'd set off towards the high ground.

The shapes of the landscape were the same as they'd been four years ago, the glitter of sun on snow as glorious as the greens and golds of summer had been. She was tempted to revel in the beauty, and the joy of having someone to share it with. These few days had demonstrated that those feelings were still present in both of them, but today there was a small voice of caution.

Two weeks was not long to get to know a person.

"Tell me about your life at sea, Philip," she said, urging the horse into a walk along the broad ridge. He'd spent over half his life in the Navy.

"What do you want to know?" His expression was wary, as if she'd asked about something she shouldn't.

"Oh, not the battles." What she could imagine of those was quite sufficient. "You were not fighting all the time, I think?"

"Hah, no. Most of life at sea is uncomfortable boredom. Damp and too hot in the tropics, wet and freezing in northern seas."

"Yet you enjoyed the life."

Alastair had talked of the satisfaction of doing his duty, but there must be many different reasons why men were drawn to the sea.

He allowed the horses to walk on, appearing to consider his words. "Part of it was the comradeship of men working together for a common purpose," he said. "But it was not only that. There is something majestic in looking out over rolling water, knowing that it stretches on for thousands of miles."

Anna shivered—that seemed frightening to her, rather than majestic.

"Too much, you think?" Philip was smiling at her, under-standing mixed with amusement, and something else. "You learn to trust in the ship and its crew. But there's beauty in the vast emptiness."

Anna watched his face as he talked about the sun sinking towards the horizon, making a glittering track of gold towards the ship; the bows creating white foam on blue water, schools of dolphins surfing on the ship's wave; flying fish, bright tropical birds, the shadows of spars and rigging against the stars.

"You miss it," she stated.

"I missed you," he replied. "Many times I wished you'd been beside me to share the moment."

She felt a rush of pleasure at his words, but it was tinged with melancholy. What she longed for was someone to share her life with, someone to love and to love her. She wanted more than just shared moments.

With Alastair she'd had companionship, someone to confide in. They'd had long discussions about art and literature, politics and history. She'd learned a lot from him, without ever feeling as though he was talking down to her.

She wanted that with Philip, if he was to be the one, as well as the intimacies and children that would come with a proper marriage.

"Have you decided yet what to do, Philip? Will you wait until they give you a new ship?"

Philip detected a wistful note in Anna's voice. She'd smiled when he said how he'd missed her, but then her expression had become more solemn.

"I'm not sure," he said. "I have been recommended to the diplomatic service." He'd talked about that with the menfolk at dinner after the ladies had left. "It is an offer I am seriously considering."

"Aren't most of the diplomats in Vienna?" she asked.

"There's always a need for competent men." He noted one corner of her mouth lift. "And yes, madam, some *do* consider me competent!"

She smiled then, her face lightening. "I'm sorry, Philip, I should not tease."

No apology was needed—he rather liked it. He knew she intended no malice.

"That will allow to you to travel, still, I suppose," she added.

"That's true. But there are other considerations as well." Such as how well he was really suited to long negotiations or remaining polite with people he disliked and disagreed with.

"I'm sure you'll make a success of anything you decide to turn your hand to."

That sounded like a compliment, but also final, as if she didn't want to discuss it further. Philip allowed the horse to walk on further, wondering if he'd said something wrong.

"Should we turn back, do you think?"

Her question made him take note of his surroundings. The advancing clouds would soon cover the sun, and the air would turn even colder.

"We can take that ridge down towards the village." He pointed with his whip. "The going should be easy on the lane from there."

She nodded, and they turned their horses. There would be other times to talk about his future—a discussion he wanted her to be part of.

"How is your life now, Anna?" he asked. Was she happy as a widow? He tried to suppress the hope that she wasn't, ashamed for even thinking it.

"Not at all exciting, compared to yours." She glanced at him and shrugged. "There isn't much to tell, Philip. There are balls in the assembly rooms twice a week, if I care to pay the subscription. Libraries, shops, a theatre. I come here several times a year."

"Is James away at school?" he asked, dredging up memories of things she'd told him.

"Yes, he boards at a school in Dorchester, but comes home most weekends, or goes to a friend's home."

"And Emily? I remember her enjoying drawing."

Anna laughed. "She does, and I am still hopeless at it. I teach her some things, but she shares tutors for drawing and music with some other girls in the town."

Emily was a little younger than James, he thought. Perhaps twelve? Anna would be responsible for her for some years yet. James, too.

He followed her into a belt of woodland, reining the hunter back to follow her along the narrow path, ducking beneath the occasional low branch.

He'd not considered her young cousins when asking her to wait for him, but at that time she had not been solely responsible for them. That had changed—could he take on two half-grown children? Looking at Anna's form, moving easily on the horse ahead of him, remembering their shared discussions and laughter, that kiss, he thought he could. He would do his best to be a good stepfather.

They emerged from the woods to find the hunting party filling the lane, and his chance for private conversation was over.

No matter—he would call on her in Weymouth, where they would not have to continually try to find a place to be alone.

He did manage to have a private moment after dinner. She'd joined him, Toby and Anthony in the billiards room, and lingered behind when the other two decided they'd played enough.

"I return home tomorrow morning, Philip. I intend to leave at first light, before the roads become too muddy with melting snow." She looked away, her fingers fiddling with the fringe on her shawl. "I'm glad we have cleared the air between us."

Cleared the air? He'd hoped they had done more than that.

"Anna." He wanted to draw her to him, but something about her stillness gave him pause. He'd hoped for a repeat of that kiss, for an indication that her hopes for the future were similar to his.

She held her hand out, but made no move towards him.

He raised it to his lips—that was not what he wanted, but he'd take it if that was all she was offering. Her hand was warm on his, but removed too soon.

"Anna, may I call on you in Weymouth?" He'd been going to ask so much more before she left, but now he dared not. He wasn't sure what had changed, but he didn't want to risk an outright refusal. That could be the end of all his hopes.

"I…" She took a deep breath, and Philip feared she was about to deny him even that. "Yes, if you wish."

"Thank you. Goodnight, Anna."

"Goodnight."

Anna gazed out of the chaise window, watching drops of rain dribble down the glass. The weather was as miserable as her mood.

Aunt Beth and her family had gathered to say their goodbyes in the hall, some still yawning. The hurt on Philip's face when her farewell to him had been a brief handshake had cut right to her heart.

The Anna of four years ago would not have done that, but she was a different person now, with different responsibilities.

Had she made a mistake last night, with that cool goodnight to Philip? It had taken a great effort not to step closer to him and accept the embrace that he clearly wanted. That she wanted too, now that the misunderstandings between them were no more.

That would be her heart ruling her head, and she was wary of allowing that. Sitting back against the squabs, she rubbed her temples.

Seeing Aunt Beth's family together had shown her what she was missing by living as a widow. The easy companionship between Beth and Thomas, and between her children and their spouses—that was what she wanted.

She could have that with Philip, she was sure.

For a while, at least. Until he started to pine for the sea or was given a new command. Then she'd turn into Aunt Pamela, waiting endlessly for letters, scanning the Gazette for news of actions in which her husband might have been involved. Might have been wounded or killed. The country was now at peace, true, but more naval men died from shipwreck and disease than in battle.

Better not to be close to him at all, than to have happiness for a short while and then lose it again.

There were her cousins to think of, too. They'd lost so many adults in their short lives. Anna suspected that the loss of Captain Severin had made little impact, as they'd hardly known him. But their mother had died, then Uncle Edward, and then the admiral. Could she introduce another man into their life who would be there for a while and then leave again?

Take a risk, her heart said, but she had more to think of than just herself.

Philip hesitated outside the open door of the breakfast parlour, not wanting to face possible questions from his aunt or cousins. He turned away—he'd have to face them at some time today, but not just yet.

"Philip."

Damn—Aunt Beth had seen him.

"Philip, wait a moment." She stood behind him, a cup of tea still in her hand.

He sighed. There was no help for it—he could not be rude to Aunt Beth.

"Come into the library." He did as he was bid, and they sat by the fire. "Now, tell me what troubles you," Beth went on, when they had settled themselves.

Aunt Beth waited. He hated laying out his feelings before another person, but he needed some advice. Badly.

"I think you know, Aunt. What I don't understand is why, or if I've said or done something wrong."

"Hmm." Beth took a sip of her tea. "What, exactly, do you want?"

"To marry her." He'd begun to want that even before Anna had finished her explanation.

"Did you ask her?"

"No." He ran a hand through his hair; Aunt Beth couldn't advise him unless he was honest. "I thought things were going well, that she might still feel for me what she did before. Then yesterday she seemed to change, to pull away."

"She wasn't happy when she left, Philip. That was clear."

"Then why did she go?"

"Why don't you ask her?"

He leaned forward and put his head in his hands. She'd given him permission to call, reluctantly. Would calling on her too soon turn her further against him?

"Have courage, Philip. I suspect she wants you as much as you want her, but I can see why she may not wish to wed you."

"Why?" He clenched his fists in frustration as Aunt Beth drank more tea, her brow creased in thought.

"When you are fighting an enemy ship, Philip, do you put yourself in the other captain's position and think about what they might do?"

"Of course."

"Well, then. It might be more difficult here, but try to think of this from Anna's point of view. What her life has been, and what it is now. And perhaps think about what you were talking of when she stopped being happy with you."

She set her cup down and stood up. "I could suggest what you should do but, to be frank, if you cannot work out at least some of it for yourself, you do not deserve to win her."

CHAPTER 9

*A*nna descended from the carriage and walked up the steps. The house looked as unwelcoming as the grey drizzle on the dull sea, and the damp air was filled with the mournful cries of gulls. She turned the key in the lock and pushed the door open.

"Excuse me, my lady." Aunt Beth's groom stood on the steps behind her, holding her trunk. She hurriedly got out of his way, and fished in her reticule for some coin. He'd got her here in record time, and now had a miserable journey back to Beechgrove.

"Thank you, my lady. I'll be off now, if there's nothing else?" He cast a doubtful glance into the empty hall.

"That is all, thank you."

Anna watched him toss a farthing at the lad holding the horses, then stepped into her house and closed the door. A faint smell of baking bread reached her—Mrs Tennant must have returned. The kitchens, at least, would be warm.

The cook was chopping onions when Anna walked in. She put the knife down and wiped her hands on her apron.

"My lady, I wasn't expecting you back so early. Joss is just lighting some fires."

"Don't worry, Mrs Tennant, I set off early." She pulled out a chair near the end of the long table and sat down. She felt drained from the jolting ride in the chaise. The same thoughts had repeated themselves throughout the journey; her head still said she'd made the right decision, but it didn't *feel* right.

"Tea, my lady?"

"Please." Anna sat while Mrs Tennant made tea and then returned to her cooking. A clatter of buckets heralded the return of Joss Tennant.

"Fire's lit in the parlour, my lady, but it's still a bit cold. I've done your bedroom as well."

"Thank you." She didn't move. It was warmer here, and the staff were used to her presence in the kitchen. She sat watching the bustle as the maids and the butler returned from their short holiday and set about their usual tasks, trying to keep her thoughts of Philip at bay.

But she could not hide from herself in the kitchen forever, and she finally asked for another tray of tea in the parlour. Settling at her escritoire, she wrote a note to the Framptons, asking them to send James and Emily home tomorrow, and sent Joss off with it. She would have to be more cheerful when the children returned.

The parlour felt bare compared to Aunt Beth's cheery rooms. The day before she left for Beechgrove she'd found some ivy to drape along the mantel, but there was not enough of it and it looked sad rather than festive. Even lighting all the candles and lamps made little difference.

It wasn't the parlour, though, it was her own feelings. Regret, and guilt, she realised, warming herself before the fire. She gazed up at Alastair's portrait, which still hung on the chimney breast. Recalling his words about the satisfaction he'd gained from his life at sea, she'd assumed that Philip felt the same. That might be true, but she should at least have asked him more about it. And explained why she'd suddenly turned cold towards him—trying to protect herself from wanting him was no excuse for hurting his feelings.

And it hadn't worked.

She couldn't go back to Beechgrove, not with James and Emily due back, but she could send someone with a letter. The irony of trying to explain herself again this way struck her as she picked up her pen, but what else could she do?

Writing the letter took some time, and involved much staring into space and several fresh starts. In the end, she said only that she regretted the way she had said goodbye, and she would be happy to see him if he would call. Dusk had fallen by the time she finished. She wrote a covering note to Aunt Beth, asking her to forward the letter if Philip had already left Beechgrove.

She drew the curtains against the night and picked up the letter. She would put it on the hall table ready to be taken to the post office in the morning. As she stepped into the hall, the knocker sounded.

Bradley walked to the door with his usual measured tread, and opened it. The man on the step wore his hat low over his face, and had a sack slung over one shoulder, but she recognised him just the same.

"Captain Kempton to see Lady Radnor."

She stared at the letter in her hand, as if writing it had conjured him up. Then Bradley stood aside and Philip entered, swinging the sack to the floor. A small pool of water gathered around him on the chequered tiles, dripping from his sodden coat and hat.

"Philip!"

. . .

Philip didn't notice Anna in the hallway until she said his name. She stood with one hand on her chest, eyes wide. Surprised, certainly, but he couldn't tell whether or not she was pleased to see him.

Assume that she is, he told himself. She looked lovely, although anxiety for the outcome of this call outweighed his pleasure in seeing her again.

He removed his hat and knocked it against his leg to dislodge the raindrops clinging to it. "May I come in? I have to say how nice it is to be coming into a warm house after such a wet journey, rather than a cold and damp ship's cabin."

She smiled, although she still appeared dazed.

"Your coat, sir?" The butler must have taken her silence for assent, and Philip readily handed over coat, hat, and gloves. His shoes had not become too wet or dirty in the short walk from the inn where he'd changed and left his saddle bags.

The butler eyed the sack dubiously. It, too, was dripping water onto the floor.

"Leave that for now," Philip said. "Lady Radnor might not want it."

The butler nodded, and bore his wet things away.

"Philip. I wasn't expecting to see you so soon."

"I hope you don't mind. You did say I could call," he added, trying to keep the uncertainty from his voice.

"I… No, of course I don't mind." She glanced at something in her hand, then back at him, her smile broadening.

That sounded promising. He picked up the sack and emptied it onto a dry patch of floor. The sprigs of holly and mistletoe, strands of ivy, spilled out across the tiles.

"What…? Where did you get all that at short notice?"

"I stole it from the library at Beechgrove," he admitted. "You may already have decorated, in which case I will gather it all up and take it away."

"Stole it…?" She chuckled, a sound that warmed his heart. "I have a little, but not enough."

Good. "We should leave it here to dry." He bent to spread the greenery out on the floor at one side of the hallway.

"Please, come into the parlour, Philip. I've asked Bradley for tea, but you may have ale or brandy if you wish."

"Tea will be perfect, thank you."

Philip paused in the parlour doorway, confronted with a portrait of an admiral in a powdered wig. The optimism he'd persuaded himself into faded a little—was the portrait still there because she missed her late husband?

She took a seat by the fire. He moved to add another log, then paused. This was her house, not his.

"Please." She gestured to the log basket. "You must be cold —your coat was very wet."

He shrugged, poking the log into place then sitting down. "I've been far wetter at sea."

There was an awkward pause. Anna wasn't even looking at him, but fiddling with whatever she had in her hand. Finally, she looked up, and held out a folded paper.

"Philip, I had just finished writing this. You can see why I was surprised to see you."

He let out a breath of relief as he read it. She *did* want to see him again.

"Why have you come? So soon, I mean."

He wanted to tell her he'd come to ask her to marry him, but that was too precipitate.

"To continue the conversation we had on the downs yesterday." He leaned forward, arms resting on his knees. "Anna, you asked me to tell you about my life at sea, and I described some of the things I enjoyed."

She nodded, her hands folded in her lap.

"I could have described other things: being in wet clothes for days at a time, the taste of water gone green from being too long in a barrel, rarely getting a full night's sleep." He sat back. "I could have said how I enjoy being ashore so I can sleep in a bed that does not move, and have a fire like this to lounge beside. That I don't mind riding through the pouring rain because I know I can get dry and warm at the end of my journey. I can have a whole—"

He broke off with a mental curse as a knock on the door heralded the arrival of the tea tray.

"I took the liberty of providing sandwiches, my lady," the butler said. Philip, eyeing the plate of food, instantly forgave the interruption.

Anna busied herself pouring the tea, her face thoughtful. Philip took a sandwich and bit into it hungrily.

"A butler worth his weight in gold," he said. "I've not eaten since breakfast."

"Philip, what was so urgent that you had to ride here in this weather?"

He put the rest of the sandwich down. This was more important than appeasing his hunger. "You were," he said. "You are. Anna, when we were riding yesterday, you seemed to withdraw from me. It was after I'd been talking about the sea."

She nodded.

"I wanted you to know that I am not wedded to a career at sea." That was possibly an unfortunate choice of words. "It is not all enjoyable, by any means."

She considered his words for a moment, her cup of tea untouched on the table beside her. "Yet that was your chosen career. The advantages must outweigh the disadvantages."

"They did." He was tempted to stop there, but he had to be honest with her. "They do still, if there is nothing else to be considered. I joined the Navy because my older brother would inherit Father's lands, and the only time I've regretted that choice was four years ago, when duty took me away from you."

She looked down at her hands, a blush rising to her cheeks. Then she met his gaze again. "You would miss the sea if you took up a different occupation."

"I would, yes."

Her mouth turned down a little at the corners; a small movement, quickly erased, but it gave him hope. He had suspected that was one of the problems.

"I wish I had my sketchbook with me," he said. "I thought of going back to my parents' house for it, but I wanted to make sure you got the greenery before the children returned."

"Sketchbook?"

"I wanted to show you some of the things I drew at sea. My box of watercolours has managed to survive all battles so far."

"Sunsets and dolphins?" A small crease of puzzlement formed between her brows. "I'm sure they are very good, Philip, but—"

"Not those. I did paint those things, of course, but I also painted from memory: the sun rising through trees on a misty morning, roses around the arch in Mama's garden, wind making waves in a field of wheat." That last attempt hadn't been too successful. Neither had his attempts to draw Anna—he could depict her features, but not the essence of her, the expressions that animated her face. "All things about the land that I miss when I'm at sea."

Anna gazed at him for a moment without speaking, wondering if she was reading too much into his words. "You miss the land?"

Philip shrugged, a wry smile curving his lips. "It sounds as if I'm never satisfied, doesn't it? What I'm making a mull of trying to say is that I'm going to resign my commission."

He stood. Her breath caught as he knelt in front of her chair, taking her hand in his.

"Anna, I love you, and I want you to be my wife. I think… I hope, that you feel the same way too."

She nodded, unable to speak.

"But there is more than love to a marriage, I think. That is why I came, to make sure there are no more misunderstandings between us."

"Philip, I'm so sorry for how I behaved last night and this morning. For saying goodbye to you in such a way."

"Don't be. You had every reason."

She hadn't, but it was lovely of him to say so. Sudden tears pricked her eyes; she could have spoiled things between them, but thankfully she had not.

"Anna." He stood, and pulled her to her feet, holding her close to his chest. She wound her arms around his waist and laid her head on his shoulder, the warmth of his embrace spreading peace through her body.

"Anna," he said again, softly, his breath tickling her ear. "You've had so many people leave your life, and you've had to be strong. You don't have to do it alone any longer."

She tightened her hold around his waist, and felt his hand stroking her back.

Anna wanted nothing more at this moment than to say yes, and let him take care of everything, but she had others to think of.

"Many of my fellow officers were married," he went on. "I always thought long absences were hard on the wives, more so than the men—at least we had our job to occupy our thoughts."

She tried to concentrate on what he was saying, not on the way she could feel his heart beating against her own.

"What if you don't like life on land?" she asked, her voiced muffled against his coat. Would he come to regret their marriage?

"I won't regret leaving the Navy. Anna, this isn't a sudden decision; it's something I've been thinking about since Boney abdicated." He released his hold and moved her away a little, gazing into her eyes. "The timing, however, is because of... of us."

She nodded.

"When you withdrew from me yesterday, was it because you want a husband who will not be away for years at a time?"

"In part, yes. But there are the children to consider, too," she added, taking a step back. The joy his words had produced would be a false one if he was expecting her to abandon James and Emily.

"I know. Anna, we have known each other such a short time. You said yourself that we don't know each other very well, so—"

"Well enough," she interrupted.

He put out a hand to stroke her cheek. "Nevertheless, if we married, I would effectively be a father to James and Emily. Don't give me an answer now, but let us spend some time together this week—you, me, and the children. I liked them when I met them at Beechgrove; I'm sure we'll rub along together well. I've taken a room at the Black Dog, and can stay in Weymouth as long as you wish."

She took a deep breath. He was right.

"That's an excellent idea."

"If we have a future together, Anna, it will always include James and Emily. They have lost enough people in their short lives."

"Thank you, Philip." She found it hard to talk past the lump in her throat. They still had much to say to each other, but there would be time for that. "Will you help me to arrange the greenery? The children will be returning tomorrow morning."

"I am yours to command."

They drank the almost cold tea, then brought in the greenery from the hall. Anna moved a stool towards the fireplace. "I'm not tall enough, Philip. Can you drape some of the ivy over the picture frame?"

He stepped up and placed ivy and sprigs of holly as she directed, but she saw his frequent glances at the painted face of her late husband.

"It didn't seem right to remove that portrait," she said, handing him another sprig of holly. "This house, all that I have, is because of him."

She stood back, regarding his handiwork critically, then placed more holly beside the clock on the mantelpiece. Working together, even on such a simple task, felt good. "That will do nicely, thank you. The rest will make a lovely table decoration."

He stepped down and moved the stool back to its place.

"He was like a father to me," Anna went on. "And a friend, but no more." She thought Philip already knew that, but she wanted him to be sure.

"Thank you for telling me." He looked into her eyes, one hand on her cheek. "It should not matter, but it does."

There was an intensity in his gaze that sent liquid heat through her body, and she stepped forward into his arms. The kiss felt as good as she remembered—no, better, for now there was also the knowledge that this was just a beginning.

Philip finally raised his head, his breathing as ragged as her own. She wanted more, but it was not yet the time for that.

"Will you stay to dinner?"

"Need you ask?"

~

The wind from the sea was cold, in spite of the pale sunshine. After several days of rain, Philip had hired a carriage and brought them all the few miles to Chesil Bank for a walk and a change of scenery. Anna and Emily had, sensibly, now retreated to the nearby inn, but James was still enjoying his new spyglass.

"Come, James. Anna and Emily will be waiting for us."

James took one last look at the frigate sailing eastwards past the end of Portland Bill, then reluctantly closed the spyglass. "Thank you for my present, sir."

"Do you really like it? It's not as powerful as the one at home." The one mounted in an upstairs room that James used to examine vessels moored in Weymouth Roads. Over the last week he'd spent some time talking to James about ships and the sea, and helping Emily with her drawing and painting.

James grinned up at him. "I know, but I can carry it around, and it's my own. Can I take it back to school with me?"

"If you wish."

They set off back towards the inn. Over the last week, he and Anna had talked of many things in the evenings when the children had gone to bed. Of his prize money, and how he might enjoy running an estate. How she and the children could visit London, or live there if they chose. Of the diplomatic service, and whether they might all live abroad. It didn't matter what they talked of—their shared glances and touches were promises for the future, and they would talk through any decisions between them, and then with the children. All of those things depended on whether she accepted his offer, of course.

Anna looked up as they walked into the inn's parlour, her lovely smile going right to his heart, as it always did.

"Sir, are you going to be our new father?" James asked.

"Do you think that's a good idea?" he asked, looking from James to Emily. If either of them said no, he'd do his best to change their minds.

"Of course it is!" James sounded almost indignant. Emily, still shy, smiled at him and bobbed her head in agreement.

But it was for Anna to answer.

"Yes, he is."

That promise of a future with Anna was the best Christmas gift he could have imagined.

THE END

Thank you for reading *Captain Kempton's Christmas*; I hope you enjoyed it. If you can spare a few minutes, could you leave a review on Amazon or Goodreads? You only need to write a few words.

∾

Find out about my forthcoming books on my website.

www.jaynedavisromance.co.uk

You can sign up to my newsletters via my website. They will tell you about new releases or special offers. I promise not to bombard you with emails. My website also has details about forthcoming books, and links to my Facebook, Twitter, and Pinterest pages.

THE MRS MACKINNONS

England, 1799

Major Matthew Southam returns from India, hoping to put the trauma of war behind him and forget his past. Instead, he finds a derelict estate and a family who wish he'd died abroad.

Charlotte MacKinnon married without love to avoid her father's unpleasant choice of husband. Now a widow with a young son, she lives in a small Cotswold village with only the money she earns by her writing.

Matthew is haunted by his past, and Charlotte is fearful of her father's renewed meddling in her future. After a disastrous first meeting, can they help each other find happiness?

Available on Kindle and in paperback. Read free in Kindle Unlimited. Listen via Audible, AudioBooks.com, and other retailers.

SAUCE FOR THE GANDER

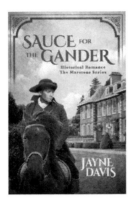

Book 1 in the Marstone Series
England, 1777

Will, Viscount Wingrave, whiles away his time gambling and bedding married women, thwarted in his wish to serve his country by his controlling father.

News that his errant son has fought a duel with a jealous husband is the last straw for the Earl of Marstone. He decrees that Will must marry. The earl's eye lights upon Connie Charters, unpaid housekeeper and drudge for a poor but socially ambitious father who cares only for the advantage her marriage could bring him.

Will and Connie meet for the first time at the altar. Their new home, on the wild coast of Devonshire, conceals dangerous secrets that threaten them and the nation. Can Will and Connie overcome the forces against them and forge a happy life together?

Available on Kindle and in paperback. Read free in Kindle Unlimited. Listen via Audible, AudioBooks.com, and other retailers.

AN EMBROIDERED SPOON

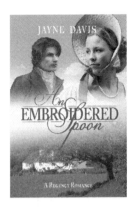

Wales 1817

After refusing every offer of marriage that comes her way, Isolde Farrington is packed off to a spinster aunt in Wales until she comes to her senses.

Rhys Williams, there on business, is turning over his uncle's choice of bride for him, and the last thing he needs is to fall for an impertinent miss like Izzy – who takes Rhys for a yokel.

Izzy's new surroundings make her look at life, and Rhys, afresh. But when her father, Lord Bedley, discovers that the situation in Wales is not what he thought, and that Rhys is in trade, a gulf opens for a pair who've come to love each other.

Will a difference in class keep them apart?

Available from Amazon on Kindle, paperback and Large Print paperback. Read free in Kindle Unlimited.

ABOUT THE AUTHOR

I wanted to be a writer when I was in my teens, hooked on Jane Austen and Georgette Heyer (and lots of other authors). Real life intervened, and I had several careers, including as a non-fiction author under another name. That wasn't *quite* the writing career I had in mind, but finally I am writing historical romance.

www.jaynedavisromance.co.uk

Printed in Great Britain
by Amazon

46215334R00068